THE SIREN'S KISS

Books by Emma Prince

Four Horsemen of the Highlands:
Ensnared by the Laird (Book 1) coming Spring 2020!
Book 2 coming soon!

Highland Bodyguards Series:
The Lady's Protector (Book 1)
Heart's Thief (Book 2)
A Warrior's Pledge (Book 3)
Claimed by the Bounty Hunter (Book 4)
A Highland Betrothal (Novella, Book 4.5)
The Promise of a Highlander (Book 5)
The Bastard Laird's Bride (Book 6)
Surrender to the Scot (Book 7)
Her Wild Highlander (Book 8)
His Lass to Protect (Book 9)
The Laird's Yuletide Bride (Book 9.5)
Deceiving the Highlander (Book 10)

The Sinclair Brothers Trilogy:
Highlander's Ransom (Book 1)
Highlander's Redemption (Book 2)
Highlander's Return (Bonus Novella, Book 2.5)

Highlander's Reckoning (Book 3)

Viking Lore Series:

Enthralled (Viking Lore, Book 1)

Shieldmaiden's Revenge (Viking Lore, Book 2)

The Bride Prize (Viking Lore, Book 2.5)

Desire's Hostage (Viking Lore, Book 3)

Thor's Wolf (Viking Lore, Book 3.5)

Other Books:

Wish upon a Winter Solstice (A Highland Holiday Novella)

To Kiss a Governess (A Highland Christmas Novella)

Falling for the Highlander: A Time Travel Romance (Enchanted Falls, Book 1)

The Siren's Kiss (A Medieval Scottish Romance)

THE SIREN'S KISS

A Medieval Scottish Romance

EMMA PRINCE

The Siren's Kiss (A Medieval Scottish Romance) Copyright © 2019 by Emma Prince

All rights reserved. No part of this publication may be reproduced, distributed, or transmitted in any form or by any means, or stored in a database or retrieval system, without the prior written permission of the author except in the case of brief quotations embodied in critical articles and reviews. For more information, contact emmaprincebooks@gmail.com.

This is a work of fiction. Names, characters, organizations, places, events, and incidents are the products of the author's imagination or are used fictitiously. Any resemblance to actual events or persons, living or dead, is entirely coincidental. V1.0

For Scott. Always.

The Legend of the Earth and the Sky
THE SUCCESSION CRISIS OF THE EARLDOM OF DRUMBURGH

1300 A.D.

To the last Earl of Drumburgh and his wife, twin sons were born on the cusp of a bright summer morning.

Roget de la Haye and his wife, Julia, had waited a very long time for a child. From the day of their marriage until sixteen years later, they had prayed for a son. The years passed and the prayers went unanswered until finally, Julia was with child. Roget cared for the woman himself, personally tending to her every need, doing everything he could to ensure that his wife and son thrived. Joy and gratitude filled the couple, spilling over into the daily lives of those who lived in the earldom, and happiness reigned. It was known as the Time of Great Joy throughout the land, a time of celebration and thanks.

And then came the birth.

Or births, as it were. Instead of one son, there were

two, and in the excitement of two heirs, the old midwife neglected to mark the firstborn son. It was a mistake that should have been paramount to Roget, but unfortunately, something else had his attention.

The loss of his wife.

The strain of the birth was too much on her weakened body, and as Julia lay dying, Roget held her hand and wept, listening to her speak of what she saw from the window of their bower, a window that faced north over the channel of the River Eden.

Julia seemed resigned to her death. She wasn't distressed, nor did she weep alongside her husband. She spoke of the world and its beauty, of the hopes she had for her sons, and of a falcon she saw soaring in the sky above the river, a falcon she was certain had come to escort her to her heavenly reward. She spoke of the gentle current of the river, and how it was much like life itself – ever-flowing, full of mystery, but never predictable.

When Julia passed, her last thought was of the bucolic and gentle river.

But Roget's grief knew no limits. When presented with his sons, healthy and screaming, it was all he could do to force himself to look upon them. Their birth, so long awaited, had killed his beloved. It was difficult not to hate the infants for what they'd done, but in the same breath, Roget knew they were a living, breathing testament to Julia. She had died to give them life and they were part of her. He named them for the last earthly visions Julia spoke of – Falcon and River.

The boys grew.

Falcon and River did not look alike, but they had much the same disposition – aggressive, intelligent, strong, and humorous. They loved one another deeply, yet there was an inherent sense of competition between them. The fact that neither one knew who was first in the birth order never mattered; they were simply brothers, and any competition between them was purely sibling rivalry.

But the birth order mattered to Roget.

Therefore, on the eve of the anniversary of Julia's death, thirty years before, Roget gathered his sons for a critical discussion. The time had come for them to determine who was to be the next earl and because of the midwife's failure those years ago, Roget had presented the issue to his clansman and they had arrived at a logical solution.

Marriage.

The first brother to marry would inherit the earldom.

Falcon and River hadn't shown much interest in marriage until that fateful day, but now, the moment was upon them. Each brother believed that he would make the better earl and now the moment had come for them to prove it. The first one to take a wife would assume the title of Earl of Drumburgh and the loser would inherit only at his brother's pleasure. He could inherit something, or nothing.

The power would belong to the heir.

Brotherly love aside, Roget's directive now pitted son against son. Each man would have to prove his worth and reach for the prize – the Earldom of Drumburgh.

But he would have to find a wife first.

Would he be foolish and take the first woman who agreed? Or would he use his common sense and realize this was not a short victory, but a life-long conquest. Fine women were rare; common women were not.

To the winner would go the spoils…

Chapter One

Summer, 1330
Arcmare Castle, Scottish Lowlands

Falcon de la Haye pushed through the double doors leading from Arcmare's great hall into the open air of the yard, his mind racing over his next moves.

He'd need a ship, but only a small one, with perhaps a one or two man crew. Hell, a wee fishing boat would probably serve his purposes. All he needed was a vessel that could cross the Solway Firth with all haste. The English town of Carlisle would only be a day's ride inland after that. And there he would find a bride.

He strode swiftly across the yard, ignoring the greetings from his father's guards as he passed. There was no time for niceties when the greatest contest yet with his twin brother River lay before him.

Falcon had to hand it to his father. Roget knew his sons all too well. He understood naught would light a fire under them quite like a competition. And he was right. Falcon and River had always measured themselves against each other, engaging in a spirited rivalry in everything from combat training to chasing lasses. With Roget's health faltering of late and no definitive heir to the Earldom, he had presented his sons with the ultimate challenge: whoever found and secured a wife first would be named the next Earl of Drumburgh.

And Falcon had every intention of winning. The title, lands, and keep were all well and good, but more enticing than the promise of the Earldom was the possibility of besting his brother in their greatest wager yet.

At this very moment, River was setting off on horseback, just as determined to win as Falcon. Where River planned to find his bride, Falcon did not know, nor did he care, for he had a plan of his own.

Their cousin Eliot, who lived north in Dumfries, had recently fought along the border against King Edward III's encroaching army. Despite the tumult of the times, he'd managed to meet and wed an English lass from Carlisle. With her sweet temperament and gentle beauty, Sarah pleased Eliot to no end. He'd brought her back to Dumfries and gotten a child on her already.

That was exactly what Falcon needed—a biddable, docile English bride to cart home with all haste. If Carlisle could produce one such woman, it could likely produce another. The border was fluid of late as Edward continued his campaign to subdue Scotland to his will. Though it was easy enough to cross, Scots were far from welcome in England.

That was where Falcon's advantage over River lay. While River plodded along overland through dangerous territory, Falcon would be gliding across the calm waters of the Solway Firth. Hell, he could even continue up the River Esk and come within a half-day's ride of Carlisle, find a biddable woman willing to become his wife, and sail home, all in a matter of days.

As he trotted down to the castle's docks, Falcon couldn't help but grin. This just might be his easiest and swiftest victory over River yet.

It wasn't until the mast on the wee fishing boat cracked, dragging the sail overboard and into the churning, black waters of the firth, that Falcon could admit "easy" might have been the wrong word for this quest.

Despite the dazzling blue sky and healthy breeze that had carried the boat onto the firth earlier that day, the weather had turned feral an hour past.

Tully, who was both captain and crew of the tiny vessel, had steered them far off course, hoping to evade the ominous purple clouds roiling toward them from the west. They'd skirted the storm, scuttling just out of its clutches again and again, but it seemed Falcon's luck had at last run out.

"Cut the lines!" Tully roared over the screaming wind. He gripped the tiller with both hands, yet the storm had long ago taken control of the boat's rudder.

Falcon battled against the lashing rain toward the tangled mess of ropes that tethered the sail to the boat. The angry waters were already pulling the broken mast and the sail away from the boat. If he didn't work fast, the entire vessel would capsize.

Yanking a dagger from his boot, Falcon set upon the lines, sawing frantically. One rope frayed and snapped, then another. The wooden planks of the gunwale to his left groaned under the strain of the dragging mast. He gripped the dagger tighter in his rain-slicked hand, severing another line.

Suddenly the boat lurched sideways. Falcon was flung against the gunwale. The air slammed from his lungs in a painful rush. This was it. The mast would pull the entire boat over, and Falcon and Tully would be swallowed by the black, churning water.

As the broken mast tugged harder at the boat, the few remaining lines tethering it to the ship went taut and slid along the gunwale. *Oh God*. Falcon was directly in their path. Before he could move, the ropes lashed tight across his chest.

He would have been hurled overboard, but his boot was wedged into something—a scupper, one of the holes in the bulwark to allow water to flow off the deck and back into the sea. As his upper body was torqued back under the force of the taut ropes, his leg remained immobilized, keeping him onboard.

But mere flesh and bone were no match for the force of the storm. With a sickening snap in his leg, his boot came free of the scupper. Less than a heartbeat later, the lines crisscrossing his chest pitched him overboard. Falcon bellowed, but the sound was swallowed, along with the rest of him, by the violent sea.

Chapter Two

Maerwynn bent to retrieve another piece of water-beaten wood from the pebbled beach. She straightened with a huff. Her apron was already nigh full of driftwood. Dropping the log into the folded wool with the others, she squinted against the glare on the glittering rocks in search of another piece.

Her gaze snagged on a tangled pile of seaweed and ropes. Much of the rope could no doubt be salvaged—one less thing she had to beg Ranulf for. She hastened her steps across the damp pebbles, but as she approached, a dark lump in the middle of the snarl became more distinct. There was cloth in the pile, and—

Hair. Dark, tousled hair, attached to a human form.

Maerwynn's grip on her apron slipped and the driftwood she'd so painstakingly collected clattered to the rocks. Fear gripped her, but just as quickly, her training took over. She'd seen many horrors in her years, but a healer did not turn away from them. If a dead body had washed onto Gull Island, then she would bury it like a good Christian. And if by some miracle the motionless figure lived, then it was her duty to help.

She hurried the rest of the way to the tangle of flotsam and dropped to her knees. With a swallow, she willed herself to look at the body.

From the firm, stubble-covered jawline poking out beneath the hank of dark hair, it was a man. And he was in one piece, from what she could tell. Maerwynn hastily cleared away the seaweed and scraps of rope. Aye, he had all his limbs, though his skin was a disturbing shade of white. She pressed a hand against his chest. To her shock, it rose and fell with breath, slow and faint but steady.

She brushed the salt-crusted locks from his face. A gash marred his forehead at his hairline. It still oozed blood. Was that his only injury? She ran her hands over the rest of his skull but found no other bumps or cuts. Continuing downward, she felt both of his arms for wounds, then pressed gently along his chest and stomach.

His clothes were in tatters, but they appeared to have once been fine. His tunic was of a tight weave and dyed a deep blue to rival the Irish Sea beyond the island's shores. Who was he, and how on earth had he come to wash up here?

She moved lower, running her fingers along his muscular thighs. His breeches, too, were stitched neatly and fit his large body perfectly. Somehow he still wore both boots, which were waterlogged but well made.

As her fingertips passed over his right shin, the man

made a noise somewhere between a groan and a growl. Maerwynn squeaked and fell back on her rump. Aye, he was most definitely still alive.

Reaching for her composure once more, she returned her attention to the leg. No blood marred his breeches, nor was the material torn, yet a few careful prods revealed that the bone was broken beneath the skin.

A curse slipped from her lips. He needed more care than she could administer here on the beach. But how in heaven was she to get him back to her cottage, which sat several stone's throws back from the shore?

She would simply have to find a way. There was no alternative. He needed her.

Bending over him, she took each one of his wrists and lifted his arms overhead. She leaned back, attempting to pull him by his arms. But besides another muffled groan from the man, naught happened.

Heaven above, he was big. And heavy. His waterlogged clothes weren't helping, but the fact was, his frame was large and powerfully built.

Maerwynn lowered his arms, considering how to proceed. Her gaze landed on the snarl of ropes around him. If she could fashion a harness of sorts, she might be able to drag him along the beach.

Separating out a long line, she wedged it around his broad chest, under his arms. Then she made a loop at the end of a short lead and fitted it low around her hips.

The fleeting image of a plow ox made her snort. She might have fetched Biddy, but the old cow was for milk, not labor, and she wasn't trained to a harness. Nay, Maerwynn was to be the work animal this time.

She leaned forward against the rope. With all her strength, she drove one leg and then the other ahead of her. Miraculously, she gained a few inches of ground. The man moaned as he slid along the rocks. At least they were tumbled smooth by the sea.

Besides, there was no helping his discomfort until she could get him to her cottage. That spurred her to take another step, then another, straining against the rope tethering her to the stranger.

By the time she'd crossed the beach and made it over the small rise upon which the cottage sat, her legs trembled and her lungs burned with each ragged breath. She let the rope go slack and sank to the coarse grass beside the man. He had not come to, but his dark brows were pinched together as if he were in even more pain.

As she caught her breath, Maerwynn scanned the beach below. From here, she could survey the entire flat, rocky expanse. No signs of a shipwreck marked the beach, but that must have been how the stranger arrived. Had the driftwood she'd been collecting come from this man's ship? Unlikely, as none of it had been fresh.

Her gaze drifted eastward to the mainland. The village of Edelby sat huddled in the alcove directly across from the island. Had he come from there? She knew all those who lived in the village. Mayhap he was passing through. But the crossing from Edelby to Gull Island was relatively short and quite safe. Nay, the man must have come from the sea beyond.

Rallying the last of her strength, Maerwynn rose and dragged the man the last few feet into her cottage. The comforting scents of lemon balm, yarrow, and an assortment of other herbs greeted her inside. Stepping out of the rope harness, she wobbled her way to the ladder at the back of the hut. Somehow, she managed to fumble her way up to the loft and pull down the hay-filled mattress she slept on.

She slid the mattress against one stone wall across from the fire, then with a mighty heave, she rolled the injured man onto it. Panting, she planted her hands on her hips and considered what to do next.

He'd need a tisane of St. John's wort to ease his pain and ward off the risk of fever, and have his head wound cleaned and possibly stitched. The worst would be setting his leg, though. She would just have to manage that when the time came.

It was a relief to set about her tasks. She knew what needed doing, and how to do it. Soon the water was boiled and the herbs steeped for the tisane. Meanwhile she'd gathered the supplies she would need to treat his head and leg.

Easing his head up, she poured the tisane down his slack throat one sip at a time. He was at last regaining his color, but she'd need to remove his wet clothing—another challenge given his large body. Hating to cut away the fine cloth with a knife, she opted instead to shimmy his tunic over his head. His bare torso was contoured with muscle. No wonder he was so damned heavy. He was lean yet stacked with strength. A warrior? Or a blacksmith, mayhap?

She pried off his boots but left his breeches for later when she'd deal with his leg. Instead she turned to the gash on his forehead. Dipping a linen cloth in a boiled concoction of yarrow and chamomile, she began dabbing at his forehead.

His brows knitted further in discomfort, but his eyes remained closed. As she blotted away the crusted blood and salt, she was relieved to find that the gash was not as big or deep as she'd initially feared. He wouldn't need stitches after all.

With the wound cleaned, she used the damp cloth to wipe the grit and salt from his face. A strong brow fell away into deep-set eyes and a straight nose. His jaw was square and defined, in strange contrast to his surprisingly soft-looking lips.

She dragged the cloth along the thick column of his neck, pondering if she should continue lower over his broad chest and corded shoulders.

When she glanced at his face again, she nearly fell back on her rump once more. His eyes were slitted open and fixed on her. They glittered like two dark, sea-washed pebbles from the beach.

Before she could gather her wits, he spoke in a low rasp.

"Are ye a siren, then?"

Maerwynn felt her eyes widen. He was a Scot, judging by his accent. He must have been blown off course and into the English coast. Unless he was a pirate or other such rogue, having sailed into hostile waters willingly.

And he thought her a siren? That she'd lured him to her and caused his shipwreck?

"Nay," she replied. "Just a woman. A mere mortal."

"Ye cannot be. Ye are not real."

His gaze was intent but clouded. Mayhap his wits were addled from his head injury, or from being tossed like a ragdoll by the sea.

Maerwynn straightened, adopting her authoritative healer's voice, the one she used with the most difficult villagers.

"You are incredibly lucky to have survived a shipwreck. But your leg is broken. I need to set it now."

Belatedly, she realized she still needed to remove his breeches. This would be awkward. Well, now that he was conscious, mayhap he could help.

She reached for the band at his waist. "Can you lift your hips, please?"

Surprise flickered in his dark eyes, followed by a predatory glint. Aye, he was most definitely a rogue. But a shackled one, at least for the moment, for when he moved to help her draw away the breeches, he winced and muttered in pain.

Maerwynn looked away discreetly as the sodden material peeled from his skin. She had treated all manner of patients, and this man was no different from the rest, she told herself firmly. Yet her face felt unusually warm as she settled a blanket over him. He was just so…male. She'd been living alone on Gull Island for too long not to notice.

Snapping her focus back to the task at hand, Maerwynn crouched at the man's feet. Just as she'd expected, his right shin was darkly bruised and swollen. Thankfully, the broken bone had not pierced the skin—less chance for the injury to turn putrid.

"This will hurt," she murmured, concentrating on the leg.

She began by prodding the area to determine the exact location of the break. The man sucked in a breath through his teeth and muttered a very Scottish-sounding curse. Undeterred, she continued inching her thumbs along his shin. At last she found the two ends of the unaligned bone.

"Blast ye, lass," he growled, his neck straining as he pushed his head back into the mattress.

Maerwynn ignored him. She pressed harder still, but neither end of the bone shifted. The broken edges must be overlapping. She'd have to reposition them apart before she could set the break.

"Brace yourself."

When the man didn't respond, she glanced up to find him unconscious, his head lolling to the side and some of the tension slackening from his face.

It was a mercy he was insensate to the world now, for this would have hurt like hell.

She closed one hand over his knee, and the other around his ankle. She drew a deep breath, then gave his ankle a sharp tug, holding his knee in place as best she could. Moving quickly, she checked the fissure once more.

Blessedly, she'd managed to not only pull the two broken ends of bone apart, but they'd slid into proper position as well. She probed the area again to be sure, but the bone now felt smooth beneath the skin.

As she bound his lower leg in tightly-wrapped linen, she let herself notice more about the man.

His legs were covered in dark hair and his feet were large, making him seem all the more coarse and rough compared to her. His big hands, which lay slack on the mattress at his sides, were surprisingly callused given his finely-made clothing. With the pain drained from his face, he looked younger, mayhap only a handful of years older than Maerwynn, though his features were still hewn into masculine lines. He was undeniably handsome.

Silently chiding herself, Maerwynn brushed away the observation and rose to fetch two pieces of driftwood from beside the hearth to fashion a brace. What did his appearance matter? It had no bearing on her treatment of him, nor on aught at all.

Belatedly, she realized she should have asked his name, where he was from, and how he'd come to wash ashore on her island while he'd been conscious. But she'd been so flabbergasted by his Scottish accent and those smoldering, dark eyes that her wits had failed her.

If her bone setting proved true and a fever didn't claim him, he would eventually wake and she would have her answers.

But until then, it seemed she was stuck with a naked, unconscious Scotsman in her bed.

Chapter Three

Falcon emerged from the murk of oblivion slowly. A low thudding filled his skull. His whole body ached as if he'd just done battle, with a particularly acute throb coming from his lower right leg.

Had he gotten into a tussle with River again? Or mayhap he'd overindulged in the de la Haye clan whisky, given his aching head.

He cracked his eyes. This wasn't Arcmare's great hall, nor his chamber, nor any alehouse he'd ever seen. The low rafters above him were hung with an assortment of dried herbs. It smelled of herbs, too, earthy and sharp. A shuttered window kept the light dim. The fire in the hearth to his right had burned low.

Where the bloody hell was he?

Memories drifted to him as if through a thick mist. His father's ultimatum to find a bride. Setting out for Carlisle by boat. The storm.

And then all had gone black—until his siren had cut

through the darkness like a ray of fiery light. Aye, a woman had leaned over him, her creamy, delicate features framed by flame-red hair. She'd spoken in a low, velvet voice before blinding pain had pulled him under once more.

But nay, that must have been a hallucination or a dream, conjured by his saltwater-addled mind. He hadn't been lured here—wherever the hell here was—by some mythical woman. He'd been pulled overboard and spit out again by the sea. Christ, he was lucky to be alive.

Just then, light and voices flooded the small room where he lay.

"…enough mugwort to take some back to the village?"

It was an Englishwoman's voice, but one he didn't recognize.

"Aye, of course," a second woman replied.

Falcon stiffened. What in…? That voice. It was the same as the woman from his dreams. Low, even, satiny —and real.

The first woman pulled in a breath. Suddenly a girl of perhaps eighteen filled his vision. Large owlish eyes blinked down at him. Her pale blonde hair had been pulled into two braids that ran down either side of her head.

"Maerwynn," she whispered, still fixing him with those rounded blue eyes. "He's awake."

Falcon heard the second woman—Maerwynn, apparently—hurry across the room. With a gentle hand on the girl's shoulder, she nudged her aside and leaned over him to take a look.

It was her—his siren, in the flesh. She studied him with ocean-colored eyes, cocking her auburn head.

"Are you in pain?"

Falcon frowned. "Aye, a wee bit, but—"

Before he could finish, she turned away. A moment later, she returned with a wooden cup of steaming liquid. Without pause, she wedged a hand under his head and lifted, bringing the cup to his lips. He sputtered on the foul-tasting concoction, but she ignored him, administering more of the warm brew.

"Blast ye, woman," he rasped when at last she withdrew the cup and he could speak again. "I'm a man grown, not some wee—"

"Can you recall your name? Where you hail from? How you came to be here?" she asked calmly.

Her imperviousness to his ire only annoyed him further.

"Aye, though I do not know where 'here' is, exactly," he retorted.

Ignoring his barbed tone, she set the cup aside and clasped her hands before her.

"You washed up on Gull Island, less than a league from the English coast."

"And ye are?"

"Maerwynn Thorne, a healer. This is my apprentice, Alice."

The thin, blonde girl hesitantly moved to Maerwynn's side. Her wide gaze told Falcon that his gruffness at least had an effect on her, if not the red-haired healer.

"And ye live here on this island?"

"I do," Maerwynn replied. "Alice lives in Edelby Village on the mainland. She comes here to study with me. And you?"

"Falcon de la Haye, first son of Roget de la Haye, Earl of Drumburgh. Or second."

Maerwynn's auburn brows drew together at his veiled comment, but she did not press for an explanation. "You are Scottish."

"Aye."

"What were you doing in English waters?"

He lifted an eyebrow at her. "They were not English when I set out from Arcmare. A storm blew me off course."

Maerwynn gave a single nod, apparently satisfied with his answers. "You are incredibly fortunate to have washed ashore here. You have a broken leg."

Falcon cautiously lifted his head. The throbbing was beginning to subside and his wits returning. Sure enough, his right leg, which poked out from the woolen blanket covering him, was bound in a brace made of two pieces of wood and several strips of linen.

"Shite," he muttered. How much time would he lose in his quest to find a bride before River? How much had he already lost?

"You've been asleep for two days," Maerwynn commented, seeming to read his thoughts. "I set the leg cleanly, but it is far from healed yet."

"I thank ye for yer ministrations," he said, wiggling his toes experimentally. It hurt like the devil, but he would just have to bear it. "I'll see that ye are compensated for yer trouble once I return home. As it is, I cannot stay."

He pushed to sitting and quickly realized he was naked beneath the blanket. Clutching it around his waist, he prepared to hoist himself to his feet.

Alice darted forward, her mouth agape. "What are you doing? You can't just—"

"Ye came from the mainland, aye?"

The girl blinked. "Aye, but—"

"Then mayhap ye can take me back there with ye. I can arrange the rest of my passage from yer village."

Flummoxed, Alice turned to Maerwynn.

"You aren't going anywhere." Maerwynn's voice was calm, yet it crackled with commanding authority. "You will require at least a fortnight of bedrest before you can even stand."

"We'll see about that," Falcon muttered. He thrust off the mattress, bracing himself for the gutting pain when he put weight on his right leg. But the pain never came, for Maerwynn grabbed his shoulder and shoved him back down.

"Are you mad, or just a fool?" she snapped. "If you stand now, you'll undo all my hard work and likely leave yourself lame for the rest of your life."

Damn it all. The lass wasn't a siren, she was a mule-headed harpy. This was precisely the opposite of what he'd set sail for England in hopes of finding—not a biddable bride, but a domineering, stubborn, intractable she-witch.

"I will not be made to stay here," he growled, pinning her with a narrow-eyed glare.

She crossed her arms under her breasts and met his glower with a testily lifted brow.

"Fine. I cannot force you. But if you leave, I will not be responsible for the damage you do to that leg."

Falcon grunted, preparing to stand once more. But her warning about permanently laming himself niggled at him.

He was strong and in his prime. Mayhap he'd done more healing in the last two days that she gave him credit for. But if he misjudged the situation, could he live without being able to walk, run, or ride, knowing it had been his own pride and impatience that had caused it?

"By all means, drag yourself to Alice's boat a quarter-mile down the beach," Maerwynn pressed. She stood there with her arms crossed, scowling at him. "Best of luck with the re-breaking of your shin bone, along with the infection that will likely follow."

With a muttered curse, Falcon sank back onto the mattress. Damn him, damn his leg, and most of all damn his flame-haired healer.

Maerwynn let out a quick, relieved breath, the first crack he'd seen in her otherwise steely demeanor. Then she turned to Alice, who still stood slack-jawed and wide-eyed beside her.

"Return as soon as you can. I want you to observe the stages of a healing bone. And don't forget the mugwort."

Alice nodded mutely, accepting the packet of dried herbs Maerwynn pressed into her hands. As the girl scuttled out of the hut, Maerwynn fixed Falcon with those incisive blue-green eyes once more.

"Now. You'll need more of that tincture to help with the swelling."

Bloody hell. It seemed that until his leg healed, he was to remain under the hellcat's power.

Chapter Four

Five days.
Five long, tedious days had passed since Falcon had woken in this cursed hut.

Five days wasted lying on his back, while time slipped away—and a full sennight since he'd set out from Arcmare. Where might River be now? Had he already won and returned to Scotland?

Falcon dug the blade deep into the sea-smoothed piece of wood he was carving. Maerwynn had given him a knife so that he might begin to fashion a crutch for himself. Likely she was as fed up with their little arrangement as he and was grateful to give him something useful to do.

Falcon was not an idle man. When he wasn't helping his father manage the estate, he preferred to be outdoors, riding, fishing, sailing, or finding new ways to test himself against River. Lying abed with naught to do but watch Maerwynn as she went about her quiet, fastidious life was nigh driving him insane.

Not that he could complain about the view. Despite himself, he had to admit that Maerwynn was a rare beauty. That wild red hair alone would have been enough to turn Falcon's head. Paired with creamy skin smattered with freckles and eyes that were as changeable as the sea, she was undeniably captivating.

Nor was her figure displeasing. Delicate curves, a narrow waist, and long legs beneath her plain wool skirts that he wouldn't mind wrapping around his hips and—

Falcon muttered an oath as the blade took a large chunk out of the wood. If he didn't rein in his thoughts, his crutch would be reduced to little more than woodchips.

It was boredom, he told himself. With naught else to do or look at, of course his gaze fell to the bonny lass living in such close quarters with him.

Fortunately, her temperament was enough to douse any lusty musings he might entertain. In the last five days, she'd proven stubborn, stern, and in possession of a willful streak to rival Falcon's.

She'd refused to let him rise except to relieve himself, and even then insisted that he hop about on his good leg to avoid putting any weight on his right side. Nor would she permit him to leave the cottage for fresh air or to assess his surroundings. He was practically a prisoner in this tiny hut, with naught to break up the long stretches of staring at the thatched roof besides the occasional administration of a foul-tasting brew he was forced to choke down.

The day could not arrive soon enough that Falcon

could leave this island and the wee tyrant of a healer holding him hostage.

As if conjured by his thoughts, Maerwynn strode through the hut door, a basket of vegetables in one hand and a bucket in the other. Seeing that he sat upright, she set both aside and crouched next to the mattress.

Wordlessly, she first checked his brace, then gently prodded his shin.

"You are healing well," she commented grudgingly. He'd told her as much every day, but she'd countered by pointing out that *he* was not a healer trained to understand these matters. "Mayhap another sennight, and you will be able to use that crutch."

"Four days."

She gave him a dry look. "This is not a negotiation."

He gritted his teeth against a retort. He would not behave like a child, even if she insisted on treating him like one. "We shall see," he said instead.

He returned his attention to his whittling, but as she moved toward the hut's door once more, his gaze snagged on her.

"What do ye *do* out there all day?" he blurted. It was late afternoon, judging from the slanted light slipping in around the shutters. As usual, she'd been in and out—mostly out—since just after dawn, when Falcon had awoken to find her climbing down from the loft at the back of the cottage.

She hesitated in the doorway, then stepped back inside.

"Well, Biddy needs milking every day," she began.

"And Biddy is…?"

"My cow."

"Ye have a cow on this island?"

"Indeed. And there is water to be fetched, and the garden needs tending."

"That's where ye get all these herbs." He gestured toward the bundles of drying plants hanging from the rafters.

As if he'd reminded her of another task, she reached for one bundle, then the next, sniffing and pinching them in some assessment he didn't understand. As she went, she rearranged them closer or farther away from the hearth.

"Herbs, aye, but there is also a plot for vegetables, and a few fruit trees as well. I have to eat, of course—and keep you fed as well."

Guilt tweaked in his gut. He'd watched her prepare several vegetable stews in the caldron over the fire in the last several days. He'd eaten heartily, murmuring his thanks, but hadn't considered that he was devouring what were likely meant to be her winter stores.

But what was more, while he'd been grumbling and simmering in his own impatience, he'd paid little attention to just how much work Maerwynn took on every day—cooking, cleaning, tending to him—all on her own. Why was there no one to share the load?

A suspicion struck him, and he found himself too curious not to give it voice.

"Do ye live alone here? Not just in this cottage, but on the island?"

Her gaze flicked to him and he noticed her neck stiffen. A strange reaction to a simple question.

"Aye."

There was clearly far more to the situation than that single confirmation offered. But she seemed unwilling to say more. Instead, she added wood to the fire, then began chopping turnips from the basket. Once diced, she dumped them into the caldron and added water from the bucket she'd carried in.

She wasn't his concern, he reminded himself as he watched her work. He was only passing through—or rather, lying about for a few more days. Curiosity about her situation did little to get him closer to his goal.

Still, some willful part of him longed to get to the bottom of the mystery that was this woman.

"Thank ye again," he said instead, meaning it. "Ye'll be paid for the trouble ye've gone to for me. I'll see to it personally once I've taken my leave—in four days."

That last wee tease earned the reaction he'd been hoping for. She sent him a withering look over her shoulder. "More like a sennight, or mayhap ten days."

"I will be long gone by then, lass. Count on it."

She began to turn back to the caldron with a roll of her eyes, but then she stilled and held him with a searching look.

"Why are you so hell-bent on leaving with such haste?"

Falcon considered how much to tell her. There was no reason to explain everything to her, but then again, he was enjoying this tentative ceasefire between them. For the moment, he wasn't growling about being bedridden and she wasn't badgering him to lie still so that he could heal.

"Do ye remember when I said I was either the firstborn son of Roget de la Haye or the second?" At her nod, he continued. "I have a twin brother, River. In the chaos of the birth, the poor midwife, who was not expecting twins, mixed us up. She could not remember which was the firstborn and which was the second. It has proven a bit of a…problem, for only one of us can inherit my father's title and lands."

Her brows shot up and she turned her back to the caldron to give him her full attention. "I imagine so."

"While not exactly ideal, it hasn't seemed a pressing issue until recently. My father's health has deteriorated—an ailment of the lungs. He fears questions about his line of succession. He wants the matter settled, and quickly. So he gave my brother and me an ultimatum—the first of us to wed would be named his heir and inheritor."

Maerwynn blinked. "So you…you are looking for a bride?"

"Aye, precisely. River set out by land, and I by sea. I'd intended to go to Carlisle, as I'd heard the Englishwomen there are docile and biddable."

At that, she snorted. "That is rather ridiculous, isn't it?"

"What?"

"You meant to collect a wife the way you would buy a cow at the market?"

"If it means I'll win, why not?"

She stared at him, confounded for a moment. "Your father's title and lands mean so much to you that you would saddle yourself with any old woman for the rest of your life?"

He leaned back against the plastered wall, considering that. "To be honest, I haven't given the title or lands much thought—nor the prospect of having a wife. But what I will not abide is losing to my brother."

"That is mad!"

Falcon shrugged. "It is our way."

"What, to seek victory over one another at any cost?"

"Aye."

At her slackened jaw and round-eyed stare, a smile tugged at his lips. "Ye must not have a brother, lass, else I imagine ye'd understand better."

Though his words were meant as a gentle jest, they had a strange effect on her. She closed her mouth and turned back to the caldron, her slim shoulders drawn tight.

"Nay, I do not have any siblings, nor any family to speak of," she muttered.

Damn him. He'd managed to turn their first light moment into grim silence with just a few words.

"I'm sorry if I've brought up something painful, lass," he offered. "I didn't mean to hurt ye."

"You haven't," she said crisply, yet she kept her back to him. "I just find it sad, that is all. Sad that you have so much, and yet…"

"What?"

She sighed, then slowly turned to face him once more. "And yet you are here." She waved a dismissive hand when he opened his mouth to object. "Not here in this hut. Of course I know you didn't intend to be blown off course, break your leg, and wash up on Gull Island. I mean here in England, spending your time searching for some woman—*any* woman—who will be compliant and meek and willing to be bound to you for the rest of your lives."

Despite the surprising tenderness he'd felt toward her just moments before, Falcon's ire stirred to life once more at her accusatory assessment.

"And according to *ye*, an Englishwoman who knows next to naught about me, what else should I be doing?"

"Spending time with your brother and ailing father!" she snapped, exasperated. "I *wish* I had a family such as yours, yet you waste the finite time you are given with them casting about in England, locked in endless rivalries and tests, competitions and challenges."

Falcon drew in a breath for a retort to put the wee hellion in her place, but to his surprise, he couldn't dredge up the words. Instead, he felt strangely deflated.

He'd never known his mother. She'd died shortly after his and River's birth. She'd used every last drop of strength to bring two strapping lads into the world before breathing her last. His father had been grief-stricken for many years. In fact, Falcon doubted Roget had ever truly healed from the loss.

What was more, the responsibilities of the Earldom did not stop just because of Roget's loss. With the dual burdens of grief and duty occupying their father, Falcon and River had been left to their own devices much of the time. They'd sought to differentiate themselves from one another by excelling under any measure—which meant constantly fighting to best each other.

There had been little softness in Falcon's life as a result. No mother's embrace over scraped knees and wounded pride, no gentle guidance or reassurance.

And no one to turn to now that the prospect of losing their father loomed like a black shadow over both Falcon and River's futures. He hadn't let himself truly contemplate what his father's death would mean. Nay, it was far easier to focus on the contest in front of him instead.

Yet somehow Maerwynn had managed to cut through all his vainglory and posturing to the heart beneath the trivial games he and his brother played.

"Forgive me," she murmured, returning her attention to the stew. "It isn't my place to speak on such matters, since I understand family so little."

"No need to apologize," he replied quietly. "Ye are right, lass. I ought to be with my brother and father." Falcon cleared his throat, but it did little to ease his sudden discomfort. "All the more reason for me to get off this blasted island so that I can find a bride and return home with all haste."

If only his damned leg would heal faster, Falcon thought. Some deeply buried intuition whispered that the longer he stayed, the harder it would be to leave.

Chapter Five

※

Maerwynn wiped her sleeve over her damp brow. The seas were calm today, the air still and warm. The sun blazed overhead, beating down on her bent back.

She'd been toiling in the garden since dawn, pulling weeds and hoeing a new patch of rocky soil. She ought to have taken a rest and eaten a midday meal by now, but she'd been dawdling over this exhausting work instead.

Coward. Not for the first time that day, the word rang through her mind. There was always plenty to do, but she needn't work herself ragged in the blistering sun. The fact was, she was avoiding returning to the cottage. *To Falcon*.

She found his presence…unnerving. His dark, incisive eyes followed her every movement, slicing through all her defenses. His large and very male body seemed to take up the entire cottage. Even when she climbed into the loft to sleep, she could sense his nearness like a breath of air that stirred the hairs on the nape of her neck.

Aye, he was intimidatingly handsome, his features and form all perfectly rugged and firm. But when he flashed a rare smile, he was somehow even more enthralling, making him appear younger and more carefree.

Thank goodness he would be gone soon. If all he wanted was to find the shortest route to a submissive, docile bride, as he'd explained yesterday, he would have to look elsewhere. Life had taught Maerwynn that there were no shortcuts, no easy paths to anything for her. Nay, it was her fate to toil here on this island, alone, forever.

Just as she bent to her task once more, her gaze snagged on the sparkling expanse of water separating the island from the mainland. A dark speck marred the dazzling blue. A boat.

Mayhap it was Alice returning for another lesson on broken bones. It would be a relief to see the girl, not only so that Maerwynn could continue with her instruction, but also to have another soul nearby to distract her from Falcon's overwhelming presence.

She lifted a hand to shade her eyes and squinted, but couldn't make out Alice's white-blonde head. All the same, she set about gathering her tools and wiping her dirt-covered hands on her apron.

By the time she glanced at the water once more, the boat had already scraped onto the rocky beach below. But as her gaze fell on the figure stepping down, her stomach plummeted.

Ranulf Swindon.

Maerwynn dropped the tools she'd collected. Lifting her skirts, she scrambled toward the beach. The garden sat on a flat plot just above and inland of her cottage. If Ranulf beat her to the hut and found Falcon inside, there was no telling how he would react—and Maerwynn didn't wish to find out. She was already walking a knife's edge here on the island, and Ranulf held the blade, as he so enjoyed reminding her.

Just as she rounded the corner of the cottage, Ranulf stepped from the rocks to the tall grass outside the hut's door.

"Constable Swindon," Maerwynn panted, smoothing her sweaty palms over her skirts. "What brings you to Gull Island?"

As he always did, he made a slow perusal of her before offering a greeting. His blue eyes slid over her face and down to her breasts. Despite the hard hammer of her heart after her dash from the garden, Maerwynn held her breath to avoid making her chest rise and fall.

Ranulf cocked his ruddy-blond head as his gaze swept over her waist and hips before eventually find his way back to her eyes. "Maerwynn," he said at last. He lifted a canvas sack off one shoulder and held it out. "I brought a few things for you."

Hesitantly, Maerwynn reached for the sack, but just as she was about to take hold, he pulled it out of her grasp.

"Tsk, tsk. Aren't you the greedy one. Not even a word of gratitude or a smile for me."

Maerwynn clenched her teeth. Ranulf enjoyed

playing these little games with her, reminding her just how dependent on his goodwill she was for even basic survival.

"I appreciate your efforts, Constable," she said tightly. "What have you been so kind as to bring?"

With a lazy smirk, Ranulf tossed the sack to the ground, forcing Maerwynn to crouch down to retrieve it. "A few ells of woolen cloth, as you requested on my last visit. Salted meat. A half-dozen loaves of bread and other odds and ends."

"Thank you," she said again, her voice wooden as she gripped the sack.

He stepped closer until he loomed over her, his frame blocking out the sun.

"You know you could have so much more than this." His low voice was like a stroke, making her recoil. But before she could stand with the bag, he pinned one corner of the canvas to the ground with his boot.

Abandoning the precious supplies was painful, but Maerwynn couldn't let him gain the upper hand physically. Releasing the sack, she stood up and took a large step backward so that his shadow no longer fell over her.

"I have already given you your answer."

Ranulf's eyes narrowed slightly. "As my mistress, you could have anything you desire."

Nay, Maerwynn thought bitterly. She couldn't have her grandmother back, nor her mother and father. She couldn't have a home or friends in the village. Ranulf had made it clear that if she took him up on his proposition, she would remain on Gull Island, alone and isolated. All he offered was to bring her more food and supplies in exchange for the use of her body.

She couldn't tell him that the prospect of being a whore, of being *his* whore, revolted her. Not when she was a mere puppet and he held all the strings. If he turned on her, she would not only stop receiving the food and supplies she could not produce herself here on the island, but he could influence the whole village against her.

Instead, she had to take a more circumspect route. "You are married, Constable," she reminded him.

Ranulf waved dismissively. "Jeanet won't let me touch her since Thomas' birth. She says she doesn't want another mouth to feed, nor to endure the risks of bearing yet another child."

That was sensible of Ranulf's wife, but it left Maerwynn in a bind. She needed a new tack, and fast given the fact that Ranulf was now moving closer.

"You, on the other hand, could benefit greatly from my attentions," he went on. "In fact, you already have. You have me to thank for all this, Maerwynn." His gesture took in the whole island. "Come to think of it, you *owe* me."

Maerwynn took another step back, her mind racing. Ranulf never failed to remind her of her tenuous position, and had even broached the subject of becoming his mistress before. But he seemed more determined than ever today. What could she possibly say to keep him at bay while ensuring her own safety for the time being?

"The village still needs my skills," she said, willing

her voice to remain even. "I do not wish for more than to remain here in peace and serve as healer to anyone in need. I doubt, however, they would look favorably upon either of us if they were to learn that you wished for me to become your—"

"Is that a threat?" he snapped, taking another step closer. He was only a few inches taller than her, yet he was near enough now that she had to look up at him. "Because if it is," he continued, his voice edged with warning, "I would not finish that sentence. You seem to have forgotten what most of the village thinks of you. That you are touched by the devil. A *witch*."

Despite her thundering pulse, Maerwynn clung to the last of her courage. "But you know that isn't true, Constable. Otherwise, you wouldn't wish to bed me. Unless you have no qualms risking the devil's touch yourself."

Ranulf's eyes widened at that, and he froze. Maerwynn swallowed. She'd finally gotten him on his heels.

Or so she thought.

"You need to learn your place, bitch," he hissed, lunging toward her.

Maerwynn lurched backward, but she'd miscalculated the distance separating her from the cottage. Her back bumped into the plastered stone wall and the air rushed from her lungs.

In less than a heartbeat, Ranulf was upon her. He pinned her against the wall with his larger body, attempting to catch her wrists. Maerwynn lashed out with both hands and knees. She landed a blow to his leg, but he caught her hands before she could strike his face.

"Submit to me, you little—"

Ranulf's low growl was cut off by a sharp clearing of the throat coming from the cottage door.

Falcon.

Impossibly, he was upright and leaning casually against the open doorframe. He held his unfinished walking stick in his right hand, but through her panic Maerwynn couldn't discern if he was wielding it more as a crutch for his leg or as a weapon.

His dark gaze was locked on Ranulf, his eyes as cold and biting as the north wind in the dead of winter. "What goes on here?"

Chapter Six

Falcon clenched his jaw against the throbbing in his right leg. Though he'd done his best not to put any weight on that side, he'd risen from the mattress and staggered to the hut's doorway with such haste that he hadn't been entirely careful.

He'd heard voices—Maerwynn's and a man's—several moments before, and had strained to discern what they were discussing. But when Maerwynn's fearful cry had cut through the hut's stone walls, Falcon had bolted upright, his crutch clenched in his hand.

What he found had sent ice into the pit of his stomach, followed by a blazing rage that burned through his veins. A man had Maerwynn pinned against the side of the cottage, his hands restraining her and his face twisted into a sneer of infuriation.

Falcon would have charged directly at the man, except that his leg screamed in protest. He was forced to use the doorframe for support, yet his grip on the crutch was some comfort—he could likely crack the man's skull with only one more step if needed.

Falcon's voice sounded surprisingly calm to his ears. "What goes on here?"

The man froze, then abruptly disengaged from Maerwynn, turning to Falcon.

"Who the hell are you?"

"Falcon de la Haye, son of Roget, Earl of Drumburgh." Falcon didn't often use the weight of his father's position to gain an advantage, but this time he put a heavy emphasis on the title, watching the Englishman through narrowed eyes.

"A Scot?" The man's gaze shot between Maerwynn and Falcon.

"Aye. And ye are?"

The man straightened and puffed out his chest. "Ranulf Swindon, Constable of Edelby."

"And what are ye doing here? I see no disturbance of the peace, except for the one ye were causing."

Swindon flushed red and his nostrils flared.

"I was discussing a private matter with Maerwynn."

Falcon's gaze flicked to Maerwynn. She'd pressed herself against the cottage stones, creating as much space as possible between her and Swindon. Color sat high on her cheekbones and fear still lingered in her wide eyes.

"The lass did not seem to be enjoying yer attentions," Falcon ground out, returning his hard stare to the Englishman.

Swindon blinked, his mouth working for a moment as he visibly fought to regain his wits. "What the hell is a

Scotsman doing on English soil, anyway?" he managed at last.

"Do ye own this island, then?" Falcon replied evenly. "I already know ye don't own Maerwynn. So why would I owe ye an explanation about being here?"

That agitated Swindon further.

"I am the Constable. It is my duty to keep the peace in this territory. A Scotsman in England would warrant further investigation. Mayhap I should even involve the Sherriff of Cumbria."

Falcon shifted against the doorframe. Though he'd like naught more than to keep needling this wee English weasel, he would do better to avoid causing problems on foreign soil. Nor did he wish to bring trouble upon Maerwynn, who would have to deal with the consequences of this confrontation long after Falcon had departed.

"I was sailing in the Solway Firth and met with a storm. I was thrown overboard and sustained an injury. Fortunately for me, I washed onto the beach of an accomplished healer." He dipped his head toward Maerwynn, who nodded tightly in return.

"Mayhap ye can clear something up for me, though, Swindon," Falcon continued, unable to avoid one more jab at the Constable. "Do all the English treat their healers with yer manners? Mayhap it is a difference in custom between our lands, for in Scotland, not only do we value our healers, but we respect our women as well."

He watched Swindon closely for his reaction. The man's lips thinned and his blue eyes filled with hate.

But there was no denying that even as a Scot on English soil, Falcon far outranked Swindon in authority and power. For now, the Constable had been cowed.

"I expect that once you are healed, you will be departing without delay," Swindon said tightly.

"Aye, ye can count on that."

"Good day, then." Spinning on his heels, Swindon stomped away. As he retreated toward the beach, he bent and scooped up a canvas bag that had been lying in the grass.

Falcon tracked him with his gaze until he'd pushed his small boat into the calm waters of the strait separating the island from the mainland and began rowing away. Only then did he let himself look at Maerwynn.

She was smoothing her hands over her dirt-streaked apron, her chin lifted but her gaze troubled as she watched Swindon's boat draw away. Her ocean eyes shifted to him.

"You shouldn't be on your feet."

Falcon's brows twitched up. "I think what ye mean to say is 'thank ye'."

"I...I was handling Ranulf."

Dark rage simmered to life once more in the pit of Falcon's stomach—not for Maerwynn, but for that bastard Swindon. "Not from what I saw."

The surge of protectiveness that accompanied his anger caught him off-guard. Aye, he would always take a stand—even on a broken leg—in defense of a woman. But Maerwynn wasn't any woman. Despite their repeated clashes and power struggles, she'd likely saved his life, not to mention his leg, and tended him like the helpless whelp he was this past sennight.

What was more, he couldn't deny that he was intrigued by her strangely vulnerable position alone on this island. Why was she here? What had happened to her family? And why exactly was her position so tenuous? It clearly had something to do with Swindon, who'd seemed to relish the power he held over her.

"I appreciate your intervention," she conceded quietly. "But you have also made matters more complicated."

"How so?"

"Ranulf revels in his role as Constable. He likes to feel in control. You made a fool of him. He might make trouble over your presence here in response."

Then it was as Falcon had feared. He had no doubt he could handle the English arse—men who picked on women usually didn't fare well when faced with someone who was their equal or better. But long after Falcon had returned home, Maerwynn would still have to deal with the lout.

"What is more, when he visits, Ranulf brings me much-needed supplies I cannot make myself," Maerwynn continued. "There is no telling when he'll return, or if he'll see fit to bring me the items I need." She let a slow breath go. "I will have to see if Alice can scrape together a few things. Either that, or simply make do without for a time."

Rigid-backed, Maerwynn moved to pass through the doorway into the cottage. It seemed she was done talking, but Falcon had more questions than ever—about

Swindon, aye, but more about her. Mostly, confusion buffeted him over her white-knuckled grasp on composure after what had just happened.

He caught her arm as she passed, delaying her. He opened his mouth to demand why she was acting so cold when he registered her trembling. *Bloody hell*. She wasn't being aloof or ungrateful—she was scared out of her wits and doing her damnedest to maintain her courage.

"Did he hurt ye?" he asked, not quite able to keep the low edge from his voice at the thought.

"Nay, I am fine," she said a little too quickly.

Without thinking, Falcon loosened his grip, letting his thumb trace a soothing pattern on her arm. "What power does he hold over ye, lass?" he murmured gently. "Does it have something to do with why ye are here on this island?"

Her gaze snapped to his, and suddenly he found himself swirling in her ocean-colored eyes. He saw fear in their depths, and longing, and sadness. Her lips parted, and he waited three long heartbeats for her to speak.

But then she swallowed and averted her gaze. "I…I am fatigued from the day's work. I think I'll lie down for a while."

Reluctantly, he let her slip out of his grasp. He rotated in the doorway to watch her walk stiffly to the ladder leading up to her loft. Though he knew he ought to look away, he couldn't help but stare at the gentle sway of her hips as she climbed the ladder, and the flash of pale, creamy ankles as she disappeared into the loft.

Using the crutch, Falcon hobbled back to the

mattress on the floor and sprawled out, staring at the thatched ceiling but not truly seeing it. Instead, the image of Maerwynn, struggling and terrified in another man's arms, was branded across his vision. He might have killed Swindon just for touching her against her wishes if it hadn't been for his damned leg. Some feral, possessive part of him wished he had.

He shouldn't care so much, shouldn't become so invested in her wellbeing when he was leaving in less than a sennight.

Yet it seemed that against all logic, his wee siren had thoroughly entranced him.

Chapter Seven

"Are you sure you're ready for this?"

At Maerwynn's question, Falcon cast her a droll look. "I've been ready for two days."

Five more days had passed since Ranulf's visit. Since then, an unspoken truce seemed to have settled between them. Falcon had acquiesced to Maerwynn's instructions that he remain abed with little more than a few grumbled words. And for her part, Maerwynn had agreed to entertain the possibility of letting him rise before a full fortnight had passed.

With only a couple of days remaining before he reached that milestone, Maerwynn had to admit that he was healing rapidly. He'd been angling to move about more freely of late, insisting that he was strong enough, and even she could no longer deny it.

He'd shocked her that day Ranulf had visited, and not just because he'd risen on a leg that had been broken a mere sennight before. The way he'd challenged Ranulf so directly, and had been so concerned for her wellbeing…that honorable, fierce man didn't square with the one looking for the fastest, easiest way to best his brother in a misguided competition. She'd almost let herself imagine…

But fortunately, she'd managed to stop herself from indulging in wild fancies. Life had proven to her that she was fated to remain alone enough times to ward off hope of a different life. She was a healer and he a patient, she'd reminded herself, naught more.

To let him test his strength and begin the process of reintroducing walking—with the aid of his crutch, of course—Maerwynn had agreed to give him a tour of the island. He stood just outside the cottage door now, impatiently waiting for her to join him.

Reluctantly, she stepped outside. Though she'd seen his improvement with her own eyes, it went against her instincts as a healer to rush things.

He must have been able to sense her hesitance, for he flashed her a roguish grin. "Don't fash, lass. If I overextend myself, ye can just drag me back to yer hut. Ye've already pulled my sorry carcass from down there, have ye not?" He pointed to the long expanse of rocky beach below the hut.

A grudging smile tugged at her lips. "Aye, I did, but I do not intend to drag you about anymore. You'll just have to ensure that you stay within your limits for this tour."

He gave her a mock bow and motioned with his crutch. "Lead the way."

Keeping her steps slow, she headed toward the garden. He kept pace with her easily and seemed unbothered by the gentle incline. When she halted beside the rows of plants, she glanced at him out of the corner of one eye to gauge his reaction.

It was a balm to her pride when his dark brows winged. "This is no kitchen garden, lass. Ye're running a veritable farm."

Indeed, she'd put a great deal of work into the plot. A healer's instincts and learning could take her far, but without a vast array of herbs and medicinal plants, she'd be hamstrung. What was more, she tried to feed herself almost entirely out of the vegetable beds, along with the few fruit trees and Biddy's milk. The less she had to rely on Ranulf for help, the less she had to fear him.

She led Falcon along the edge of the herb beds and past the vegetable plots. Biddy lifted her head and glanced at them as they passed her pen before returning to contentedly munching her cud.

"This was all rocks and grass when we arrived ten years past," she said, gesturing at the garden.

"We?"

Maerwynn hesitated. Her pride had led her to say more than she'd intended. There was no reason to expose the wounds of her past to Falcon. He'd made his desire to be gone as soon as possible abundantly clear. What was the point in opening up to him when he would just leave?

Then again, saying nothing now would cast an awkward air over the rest of their outing. And Maerwynn couldn't deny that she was enjoying this afternoon with Falcon.

"My grandmother," she said cautiously. "We came

here together and started the garden. The foundation of the hut was already here—a fisherman had once lived on the island—but we restored it to its current state."

"Where is she now?"

As it always did when she thought of her grandmother, Maerwynn's chest tightened. "She died. Four years past."

She cast him a glance and saw his features tighten as he drew the obvious conclusion. *Aye, I've lived here alone for four long years*.

"I'm sorry for yer loss," he offered, falling silent for a moment. "What inspired the two of ye to make yer home here?"

Maerwynn quickened her pace slightly. "Oh, the usual reasons. Here is the stream that provides the island's fresh water."

Thankfully, Falcon didn't question her further as they fell in alongside the stream and began to ascend further.

The ground grew steeper and rockier as they continued up, with the shrubbery falling away and craggy outcroppings taking their place. By the time they reached the island's highest point, Maerwynn was grateful for the breeze coming off the water. She let it cool her as she caught her breath.

Falcon seemed unfazed by their ascent. His broad shoulders were held straight and his chest rose and fell with steady breaths. Healthy color sat on his defined features, and his dark eyes sparkled not with fatigue but verve.

She was only watching him so closely to make sure

his leg fared well, she told herself firmly. Not because the sun caught his dark hair and made it shine, nor because of how alive and invigorated he seemed at the chance to be outdoors.

He turned in a slow circle, taking in the whole of the island. "It is smaller than I thought," he commented. "Ye could walk the entire circumference in three quarters of a day."

Indeed, Maerwynn had done just that many a time.

His gaze landed on the island's northern slope. The rocky ground fell away into a rugged cliff face. Hundreds of white gulls spiraled through the air. They swooped into the cliff, pulling up at the last possible moment to roost in the innumerable crevices and nooks in the rock.

"I see now why it is called Gull Island."

"They make their nests in the cliff face. During nesting season, they gather in such numbers that they can be seen from Edelby."

Falcon's gaze traveled across the strait to the mainland, where Edelby's huts appeared as specks against the green shoreline. "Are ye from Edelby then?"

Like a dog with a bone, it seemed he would not let go of his curiosity about her, no matter how she tried to evade his questions.

"Aye."

She felt his eyes on her, dark and searching. He tried a different tack.

"I must admit, I am impressed. The cottage, the garden—ye've made a great deal out of this hardscrabble island. Yer hard work is to be commended, lass.

But I cannot help wondering if it isn't a lonely life. Why not just live in the village?"

Maerwynn felt her shoulders stiffen. "I think that is enough exploring for today. You've pushed that leg far enough. We'd best—"

"Maerwynn." Her name was a soft caress on his tongue.

She forced herself to look up at him, steeling her spine for his perceptive gaze. But the depths of his eyes were not cool and analytical. Instead, they were shockingly warm. He slowly traced her face, his gaze settling for a moment on her mouth before returning to her eyes.

"I didn't mean offense, but I find that I am…curious about ye. Invested in yer welfare."

Was he…did he *care* about her? Nay, he hadn't said that much. *Foolish girl*. Just because she found herself drawn to him didn't mean he felt the same.

But the way he kept staring at her, like he longed to devour her on the spot…

Her fascination got the better of her. Just one touch, just to see if his reaction echoed her own.

She reached out slowly, her fingertips barely brushing over his stubbled jaw.

To her astonishment, he shuddered, but instead of pulling away, he took a swift, jerking step toward her. One rough, warm palm closed around her cheek, his thumb tracing her lower lip. A shiver jolted over her skin, traveling over every inch of her like ripples over the surface of water.

"Tell me I can kiss ye."

A breath slipped from her suddenly slack lips. "A-aye."

Instantly, he tossed his crutch aside. It clattered on the rocks at their feet, but Maerwynn hardly noticed, for in the next heartbeat, he'd tilted her chin up and settled his lips over hers.

Maerwynn's mind scattered in a thousand directions. It felt as though the whole island tilted on its side. All she had to anchor her through the kiss were her senses.

He was all contrasts. Coarse stubble and surprisingly soft lips. The gentle pressure of his mouth and the firm grasp he'd taken on her waist. Her hands fluttered to his chest. The taut strength in his body was unmistakable, yet so was the drawn restraint in his power.

He brushed the seam of her lips with the tip of his tongue, wordlessly asking entrance. So baffled was Maerwynn that she complied on instinct alone. She wanted more of this kiss, more of him. That imperative thrummed through her like a swelling tide.

The heat of his mouth as it fused with hers sparked a fire deep within her. It was unlike aught she'd felt before—so intimate and consuming.

She surrendered to it, letting one sensation chase the next as he deepened the kiss further. Their tongues twined into a slow velvet caress, setting her pulse thundering in her ears. One of his hands tightened in the hair at the nape of her neck. Distantly, she realized her own hands had turned to talons on the front of his tunic.

Abruptly, Falcon drew back, his breath coming short and his dark eyes glazed with hunger. He stared at her, seemingly as stunned by what had just transpired as she was.

Maerwynn fumbled for something—anything—to say. That the kiss had been a mistake, mayhap, but the trouble was, it hadn't felt like a mistake. Nay, it had felt like the rightest imaginable moment.

A flicker of movement over Falcon's shoulder caught her eye. A boat was crossing the strait to the island. He must have noticed her diverted attention, for he turned and followed her gaze.

"That had best not be Swindon again," he practically growled.

Maerwynn squinted. From this height, she could make out two people on the small boat, one with blindingly white-blonde hair, and another with a long brown braid.

"Nay. It is Alice and likely a woman from the village. Alice probably brought her here because she needs healing."

Which meant that Maerwynn was saved from having to make sense of what had just passed between her and Falcon—at least for the time being.

Chapter Eight

By the time they reached the hut, Alice and the village woman had already crossed the beach and were waiting outside.

Alice's owlish blue eyes widened when they landed on Falcon as he crutched his way after Maerwynn. No doubt she was surprised to see him upright. If he were honest, Maerwynn had been right when she'd said he'd overtaxed himself. Their stroll around the island had been invigorating. And their kiss…he'd damn near forgotten his leg completely when he'd felt her mouth beneath his.

But the walk back down to the cottage had left him clenching his teeth. He'd never admit it, but he was grateful for the chance to sit upon his mattress once more.

And watch Maerwynn work.

"Beatrice," she said, greeting the villager.

The woman was of middling years, her thick brown braid streaked with gray and her build sturdy from a lifetime of hard work. She wore a wary scowl as she nodded to Maerwynn. Then her gaze flicked to Falcon.

"Another patient of mine," Maerwynn said by way of explanation. "Come inside, everyone."

Falcon followed the women in and sank gratefully onto his mattress. Meanwhile, Maerwynn launched into a series of questions for Beatrice about what was ailing her.

"I cannot be rid of this cough," Beatrice answered. To illustrate her words, she gave a few dry hacks that made her hunched shoulders shudder.

"I gave her a tisane of steeped horehound a few days ago," Alice interjected, "but it doesn't seem to be helping much."

Maerwynn tapped her chin for a moment. "Horehound is the correct remedy, but mayhap a brew that merely slides down the throat isn't enough. Hardened drops of distilled horehound and honey that can be sucked for long stretches should do the trick."

She set about the cottage gathering various jars and pulling down a clump of hanging herbs. Alice helped Beatrice sit on one of the wooden stools in the corner, then moved to Maerwynn's side to assist her.

"Add water and three stalks of horehound to the caldron," Maerwynn instructed, withdrawing a lid from what was apparently a honey pot.

Once Alice had seen to her task, Maerwynn added several generous dollops of honey to the caldron. She turned to eye the other herb bundles dangling from the rafters, then after a moment of consideration, she removed a few leaves from another dried stalk.

"Lemon balm," she murmured to Alice, "to soothe a raw throat, and for taste." She added the leaves to the caldron, then took up a wooden spoon and stirred the concoction slowly.

The cottage filled with a sweet, herbaceous scent that Falcon found pleasing. But when he glanced at Beatrice, she was casting a narrow-eyed stare at Maerwynn's back.

What the hell was wrong with the woman? Maerwynn was hard at work on a remedy for her cough, yet Beatrice was looking at her like she had devil's horns sprouting from her head and a forked tail snaking out from her dress.

For her part, Maerwynn seemed not to notice—or if she did, she paid Beatrice's ice-cold looks no mind. She carried on stirring, occasionally giving Alice some quiet instruction or insight into what she was doing.

Once the mixture in the caldron reached a boil, she tipped it carefully into a flat cast iron pan, which she placed directly onto the fire beneath the caldron. After a few minutes, the concoction began to thicken and bubble in the pan, turning tacky and then solidifying.

Using the edge of her apron, Maerwynn lifted the pan from the fire and set it on the wooden table beneath the window to cool.

"How do Brenna and Theo fare?" she asked, turning to Beatrice. "Last I heard, Brenna was soon to be married and Theo was working John Welton's land until his own son was recovered from his fever."

"My boy came home weeks ago," Beatrice replied sourly. "And Brenna has already wed the butcher's son."

"Ah," Maerwynn said, her voice faint. "It seems I am behind on the news then."

With the attempt at small talk so thoroughly shot down, an uncomfortable silence fell over the hut. Beatrice cast a few more glances at Falcon, but for the most part, she pretended that Maerwynn wasn't standing right in front of her. She kept her gaze fixed on some spot on the thatch ceiling above all their heads as she waited.

At last, the awkwardness was broken as Maerwynn retrieved a wooden mallet and a cloth from a cupboard. She wrapped the mallet head in the cloth, then thwacked the now-hardened contents of the pan with it. The concoction cracked and broke apart into pieces, which Maerwynn collected in the cloth.

She extended the little package to Beatrice, who took it with a frown.

"Suck on a piece until it dissolves—several a day if needed. And come see me again in a sennight if the cough hasn't improved, or if you run out of the drops."

When Beatrice gave her only the barest nod of acknowledgement, Maerwynn glanced at Alice.

"I'll check in on her and make sure she returns if she grows worse," Alice said quickly.

"Good."

Without a word of thanks, Beatrice rose and shuffled out of the cottage, Alice trailing behind her. Alice cast an apologetic look to Maerwynn before closing the door after them.

Falcon sat in dumbfounded silence for a long moment after they'd gone. Maerwynn's spine was as straight as ever as she set about cleaning the pan and caldron, but Falcon didn't miss the tension around her blue-green eyes as she bent to the chores.

"What the bloody hell was that?" he blurted at last.

Maerwynn glanced at him. "What?"

He pointed to where Beatrice had been sitting. "That. Good God, ye'd think the woman suspected ye of giving her poison rather than a remedy for her ailment. She was glowering at ye the whole time, and never once thanked ye for yer help."

Maerwynn huffed a humorless breath. "She very well may have considered if it was poison."

Falcon crossed his arms and shifted on the mattress. "I do not understand. Why would she treat ye like that—cold and ungrateful?"

"Some of the villagers…do not like coming to the island."

"It didn't seem to be the island that bothered her, but *ye*."

When she continued scrubbing the caldron without responding, Falcon let out a breath.

"Maerwynn, why don't ye just tell me what is going on? What harm could it do?"

Chapter Nine

What harm?

Don't open yourself to him, a voice whispered in the back of Maerwynn's mind. *Don't show him your vulnerability. Don't allow yourself to care.*

If she let him draw close, it would be that much more painful when he left in a few days. Everyone always left. And she would be consigned to pick up the pieces alone.

Yet she had already crossed that line, hadn't she? Aye, she'd gone tumbling headlong over it with that searing kiss.

Besides, it was clear he wouldn't let the matter go, and she was tired—tired from dealing with Beatrice, tired of evading his questions, tired of always keeping her chin up and her back straight.

"I grew up in Edelby," she began, slowing in her scrubbing of the caldron. "My mother and father and grandmother all lived on the outskirts of the village. My grandmother was the village's healer. She came from a long line of healers—she always said the gift was passed down through the women of the family. It skipped my father, but she believed the line was continued in me."

"She taught ye the healing arts, then?" Falcon surmised.

Maerwynn nodded. Her mind drifted back to those idyllic years—days spent in the small shed behind her parents' house with her grandmother, the smell of earth and herbs and wildflowers filling the air. She had watched with rapt attention as her grandmother showed her all the uses for the plants and all the ways to transform them into medicines.

Those happy years had come to an abrupt end all too soon.

"My mother and father both died within a few months of each other when I was ten. My father was killed by roadside thieves on his way to Keswick to buy supplies my grandmother couldn't grow herself. And my mother was taken by an overpowering fever not long after. We did everything we could to save her, but my grandmother said God's plan is more powerful than any medicine."

Falcon's jaw flexed as he swallowed. "I'm sorry, lass."

She sank back on her heels for a moment, stilling. "It was a terrible blow at the time, of course, but I still had my grandmother. She made me her assistant, and the work of healing others helped ease my own pain."

"What made the two of ye decide to come to the island?" he prodded gently.

Maerwynn's stomach involuntarily knotted. It was time to venture into the deepest wound of all.

"When I was fourteen, a terrible plague swept through the village. Nearly everyone fell ill, and fully a third of the village perished."

She closed her eyes for a moment against the memories of the bodies piling up outside their neighbors' doors, the flies, the stench, and the wails of those who'd survived only to lose their entire family to the pestilence.

"Everyone lost someone. Whole households perished. My grandmother and I did what we could, but…" She shook her head, swallowing hard.

"Maerwynn."

Through blurry eyes, she looked up to find Falcon's hand extended toward her. She rose on shaky legs and crossed the room, letting him pull her down to sit beside him on the mattress.

"I haven't known ye long, lass," he said, keeping her hand folded inside his. "But I know ye well enough to be sure ye did everything in yer power."

Maerwynn nodded, blinking away the moisture from her eyes. "We worked tirelessly, but there were so many in need. Yet we could offer little besides a small amount of comfort in most cases. When at last the plague began to wane, the whispers started up."

"Whispers?"

"A few of the surviving villagers mentioned that death seemed to follow us. It was only because so many fell ill that we had to pay a call to nearly every home in the village. And the pestilence moved so quickly that many died within hours of our visit. But some were suspicious of the fact that neither my grandmother nor I ever became sick, despite touching and breathing the air of the dying."

Falcon's face darkened and his hand tightened slightly around hers. "Ye mean to say…the ungrateful bastards *turned* on ye? After all ye'd done for them?"

"Grief blinded them," she murmured. "They wanted someone, *anyone*, to blame."

"Ye do not need to defend them," Falcon said, his voice low and drawn. "What did they do to ye?"

Maerwynn gathered her composure as best she could. The past was done and gone, she reminded herself.

"The word 'witch' was whispered, then spoken aloud. Some said we were touched by the devil. Others defended us and urged the rest to be reasonable, but mostly there was simply so much confusion and fear in the aftermath of the plague that some solution was demanded."

Falcon tensed. "And that solution was?"

Unbidden, fear once again crawled up Maerwynn's throat. "There were calls, albeit only a few, to burn us so that the village would be rid of the evil that had caused so much suffering. But a few loyal friends and neighbors spoke vehemently against such an extreme act. It was Ranulf who suggested a compromise—exile to Gull Island."

"Swindon?" Falcon snapped.

"Aye. His father had been Constable, but the plague claimed him as well. He was eager to step into the role and reinstall order in the village in the plague's aftermath. My grandmother and I had little choice—it was either let the villagers put us to the flames or leave our life behind and start over here."

Falcon snorted softly. "Let me guess—he thinks ye owe him now for saving ye."

She glanced at him, surprised at his astute insight. "Indeed. And he…*wants* things of me in exchange."

At Falcon's low noise of anger, she hurried on.

"But dealing with him is still better than the alternative. My grandmother and I agreed to remain here and avoid trouble, and also provide our skills to anyone from the village willing to associate with us. Most are still wary, but they will accept my help if they truly need it."

Another realization flickered across his features. "That explains Beatrice's abominable behavior toward ye. Do they still fear ye, then?"

"Aye, some do. That is why I began training Alice two years past. She sees to most of their ailments, and despite the fact that she is my apprentice, the villagers don't seem suspicious of her the way they are of me." She ducked her head. "And it is nice to have the company from time to time, now that my grandmother has passed on."

Falcon leaned back against the plastered wall, a considering frown knitting his brow. Maerwynn glanced down at their still-entwined hands. He was absently stroking her palm with his thumb. He seemed unaware of the soothing gesture as he contemplated all she'd said. A small thrill chased through her. Warmth blossomed from their point of contact over the rest of her skin as she waited for him to speak.

"I am confused about something," he said eventually. He turned to her, the frown still fixed on his face. "Why have ye remained here all these years? Aye, I understand why ye cannot return to the village, and even why ye'd want to stay with yer grandmother. But after all ye've lost—and all those damned villagers have taken from ye—why wouldn't ye just leave?"

"It isn't that simple."

"Isn't it? Of course, it would take some work, not to mention coin, but ye are resourceful. Ye could trade yer skills for safe passage to a new town. There must be a thousand other places that would be grateful to welcome a talented healer."

Maerwynn averted her gaze. "I made a promise to my grandmother when we moved here. Aye, some in the village had mistreated us, but that didn't give us the right to abandon them. She always believed the healer line in our family was a gift from God. It would be wrong to withhold that gift, to deny the villagers the care they needed, no matter if they were friend or foe. She asked me to promise never to leave them without my gifts. And I did."

"But ye deserve to be happy," he retorted. "To be valued and cherished. Ye deserve the world, Maerwynn."

Her heart gave a painful lurch at that. *Don't, Maerwynn. Don't let yourself fall.*

"I can't," she whispered. "I can't break my promise, nor abandon those who need me."

And I can't let myself care for you when you will only leave, just like everyone I've ever loved.

Chapter Ten

※

Falcon swung the axe with all his might, sending the log splintering beneath it.

It felt good to exert himself, even though his right leg still ached a bit under the tightly-bound linen bandage. Still, he was upright, his brace removed and his crutch lying in the grass next to him. His right foot rested on the ground, the slightest bit of weight borne on that side a sign of all his progress.

He should have been elated. He should have been planning his next move—how to get off the island, followed by arranging passage to Carlisle, then Arcmare, bride in tow.

Instead he was chopping wood like a madman beside the stream. He'd been at it since shortly before dawn, when the sky had been only a few shades lighter than the surrounding sea.

Before that, he'd lain awake on the straw-filled mattress, fighting every instinct screaming at him to pull himself up the ladder and into Maerwynn's loft. *Into Maerwynn's arms.*

He finally had the whole story from her, the reason she was here alone and why she would not leave despite all she'd been through. It should have satiated his curiosity, scratched the itch he'd felt ever since he'd opened his eyes to behold his ethereal siren.

Yet their conversation had left him restless and ill at ease. Against his will, he found himself pulled to help her in some way, to linger a little longer in hopes of easing her burdens.

That was why he'd eventually risen and slipped out of the cottage to chop wood. At least he could help her in this simple, physical way.

But that was only part of it. He hadn't realized until the wee hours of the night, as he'd chewed over all she'd said of her past, that he had completely forgotten to speak with Alice about getting to the mainland. Aye, he wasn't fully healed yet, but now that he no longer needed the brace and could move about with the aid of his crutch, he could presumably depart under his own power.

He could tell himself that he'd forgotten because he'd been fatigued from his tour of the island yesterday, then confounded by Beatrice's strange behavior. But that was a lie.

The truth he didn't want to admit was that some part of him was reluctant to leave. That was the real reason he was out here chopping wood as if he were preparing for a hundred bonfires. It was easier to waste himself in mindless exertion than dwell within his own thoughts and feelings.

He couldn't deny it, at least not within the privacy of his own mind—he'd come to care for Maerwynn. Learning of her past and all that she'd overcome had only intensified the feelings that had already begun to take root within him.

She was smart, and capable, and stubborn, aye, but that was because she knew what she was about. And she was so bonny that it made him ache whenever he wasn't touching her.

But she wasn't for him. And not because she was as far from a biddable, docile bride as the sun was from the moon. Nay, it was because her life was here, and his was in Scotland.

She was determined to remain as Edelby's healer, no matter how they mistreated her. Yet thanks to her, Falcon felt the pull of home, of family, stronger than ever. He didn't want to waste any more of his limited time with his father and brother gallivanting about on some foolish quest to prove himself his brother's better. And she'd been the one to inspire such a change.

He should never have involved himself with Maerwynn, never let his curiosity grow, or his admiration, which had now deepened into something far more profound. But it was too late for that. So here he was, swinging an axe as though it would solve his problems, hoping against hope that he could leave without breaking her heart—or his own.

"Falcon?"

Despite the fact that he'd been ruminating on her all

night and into the morning, the sound of Maerwynn's distant voice sent a warm jolt of surprise through him.

"Up here."

She came around the corner of the hut, a knitted shawl clutched around her shoulders against the mild morning. When she spotted him beside the stream, she hastened her steps toward him.

"What are you doing?" she asked, her gaze taking in the axe in his hand and the substantial pile of firewood off to one side before shifting back to him. Her eyes slid over his bare chest in a slow perusal.

Despite the cool breeze blowing off the water, he'd grown warm as he'd worked the axe and had doffed his tunic. Now he was getting hot again, but it had naught to do with his earlier exertion.

"I thought I could be useful for once, instead of a burden." He offered a half-smile, propping the axe on the ground. "I didn't wish to wake ye by chopping right next to the cottage, so I came up here."

"You shouldn't be overextending your leg when you've only just—"

He held up a hand to placate her. "I haven't been putting my full weight on it. And I am only a day shy of a fortnight since the break. Ye said once the brace was off, I should move about a wee bit to ease the leg back into use."

Her auburn brows pinched, but she couldn't refute her own advice to him.

"I'm glad ye're here," he said slowly. That was true enough, but what needed to be said next would not be easy. "Now that I can stand and get around with my crutch, I am not bound to remain on the island."

A cloud passed behind her eyes. "Aye."

"I was thinking…that is…" He drew in a steeling breath. "I plan to accompany Alice to the mainland the next time she visits."

When she remained silent, he hurried to fill the void.

"I should have done as much yesterday, but Beatrice's presence and my own fatigue distracted me. Besides, another day's rest seemed in order. But now there is no reason for me to stay."

Aye, no reason. Only emotion.

"I see. And you plan on continuing your mission to find a willing bride to take back to Scotland with you?"

"Aye."

Her chin remained lifted and her features serene, yet the hands clutching her shawl had turned white around the knuckles. "Very well. As your healer, I would advise you to keep the leg tightly wrapped for several more weeks, and introduce weight and activity slowly to prevent re-injuring the bone while it is still healing."

"Maerwynn." She had taken on a cool, practical air to protect herself, he knew—to protect both of them. Yet Falcon couldn't stand the thought of this being the way things would end between them—with a few formally spoken words of advice and naught more.

She looked up at him with eyes like a storm-tossed sea. He couldn't help himself then. He reached for her, dragged her against his bare chest, and kissed her.

She went soft in his arms, yet her kiss was filled with as much urgency as his own. Her tongue sought his for a satin caress. Small hands slid over his enflamed skin, searching, clutching him closer.

He hauled her tighter to him, crushing her delicate curves into the unyielding planes of his body. Yet he wanted her closer. Their mouths still fused, his hands slid under her shawl, nudging it off her shoulders. His hands roamed over her slim back and around her waist. He could feel her ribs straining against her wool gown with each of her ragged breaths.

Heaven help him, he ached to yank the laces running down her back loose and peel the damned garment from her body. He needed to touch her, skin to skin, to taste her, to drive inside her.

With every last drop of self-control, he pulled his mouth from hers, breaking their kiss.

She stood before him, dazed and panting, a look of frustrated desire written clearly on her bonny face.

"We should stop," he breathed through gritted teeth. Despite his words, his betraying hands still hadn't fully released her. He gripped her waist as if she were an anchor in a storm. Yet touching her only made the tempest inside him rage all the more powerfully.

"Why?"

Her direct look and the simple question shook him to his core. Bloody hell, he wasn't strong enough to resist the pull he felt toward her.

"Because I want so much more than a kiss," he rasped. "I want to strip away yer clothes and lay ye out here on the ground. I want to explore every last inch of ye with my hands, my lips, my tongue. And I want to take ye completely, be inside ye, fill ye."

As he continued, her lips parted and a rosy flush bloomed over her cheeks. But her sea-swept gaze held his, unflinching.

"And if I want the same?"

Falcon sucked in a breath. She couldn't mean it. Yet still she did not break their stare.

"If we do this, it will not change aught," he murmured. "I will still leave."

"And I will stay here. But at least I will have shared this with you." Maerwynn's voice drew taut and low with emotion. "At least I will not regret what little time we have left."

To dull the terrible ache that pulsed in his heart, he closed the distance between them. There was no going back now.

Chapter Eleven

※

Maerwynn welcomed the sensation of falling as she surrendered completely. But just as quickly as she went tumbling over the edge and into the unknown, Falcon was there to catch her.

His arms were like bands of steel as they closed around her. When his lips met hers, she kissed him with fierce abandon. She would never regret this, no matter the prospect of many long, lonely years stretching ahead of her. Even in those dark times, she would have the memories of this moment to warm her.

Falcon dragged his mouth down the column of her neck, sending shivers along her skin. He fumbled with the ties running the length of her back. He was truly going to make good on his promise to strip her bare. And then…

Anticipation surged like a hot wave through her veins. Though her life was a lonely, isolated one, the single silver lining was that she answered to no one. She could make her own choices, and this was what she wanted, what she chose—a sliver of joy for herself, albeit fleeting.

As the ties on her gown came loose, she sank her fingers into his taut back. He dipped lower when the wool sagged off her shoulders, trailing kisses across her chest to the edge of her linen shift. And when his lips moved lower still to brush the pebbled peaks of her breasts through her shift, it felt as though a bolt of white-hot lightning forked through her.

Unbidden, a breathy moan escaped her throat. He murmured a sound of low approval and intensified his attention on her breasts, one hand caressing her while his mouth teased and plucked against the linen.

A whisper of cool air swirled over her enflamed skin, and she realized he was easing her shift away. She let it fall without hesitation, eager for naught to separate them. The sun was warm on her hair and bare back, the air cool and sharp with salt. Standing naked, she had never felt freer.

Nor more beautiful, for Falcon was staring at her as if she were a goddess in the flesh. His gaze roamed hungrily, reverently, over her.

"Ye are the most bonny thing I have ever seen," he murmured, swallowing hard.

Hastily, he snatched his discarded tunic from the ground beside him and snapped it out, then draped it over a particularly soft-looking patch of grass right next to the burbling stream. Taking her hands, he drew her down onto it and eased alongside her.

He kissed her cheek, then her chin, then her neck, light as the wings of a butterfly. He burrowed through her hair and nipped her earlobe, making her gasp. And when he returned his lips and tongue to her breasts, her head lolled back and all she could do was cling to him.

He moved lower still, scattering kisses across her ribs and stomach. Then he eased her legs apart with a little nibble on each thigh. She opened to him, lost to the swelling sensations.

But they were naught compared to what came next.

She bowed off his tunic when his mouth closed over her most intimate flesh. Flames scuttled through her as he licked and caressed her, building until her whole body was afire with need.

"Falcon," she hissed. "Please." She didn't know what she was begging for, but she was certain he could give her what she so desperately craved.

He rose up, fumbling frantically with his breeches. She watched in enthralled fascination as his manhood sprang free, hard and thick with his arousal.

He was forced to slow as he drew the fabric over his right leg, exposing the linen wrappings around his calf and shin. She didn't mind, for it gave her more time to marvel at his body.

She'd seen the male form plenty of times, but none was as commanding or entrancing as Falcon's. Just as when she'd first laid eyes on him, she was struck by his raw muscular power. Every inch of him was hard and honed. Where she was soft and rounded, he was all solid planes and angles. They were a study in contrasts, and yet she knew instinctively that they were made to fit together.

As if to prove just how true that was, he eased

himself between her legs. As his manhood brushed her entrance, he held her gaze.

"Are ye ready?"

"Aye."

With deliberate restraint, he slowly pushed into her. His head sank beside hers and he breathed words in a tongue she didn't understand—Scots? Gaelic?—against her ear. She let them wash over her, absorbing his reverent tone if not the words' meaning.

Soon she was gulping air and struggling to accept more of him. But he waited for her, holding still until her body grew used to the invasion and she relaxed a hair's breadth.

When he was buried fully within her, one hand found her breast, the rough pad of his thumb circling its peak. The pleasure from before rushed back like a flood, replacing the lingering pain and discomfort.

He began to move, slowly at first, letting her gain the rhythm and the wave of sensation that followed it. Then when her hips began meeting his, he sped, thrusting harder, claiming her completely.

His hand slipped between them, finding that point of pure pleasure he'd caressed with his tongue earlier. Suddenly it felt as though a dam was breaking within her. Ecstasy swept her away, stealing her breath and wracking her whole body with shudders of pleasure.

Her release set off his own. He drove into her, holding himself deeply as his body went taut. He growled her name as he shook and strained, then sagged over her, spent.

Though drowsy satisfaction settled like a fog over

her, a sense of emptiness stole through her as he eased down to the grass beside her. He drew her against his chest, holding her close, yet it wasn't close enough. And all too soon, he would be gone completely.

She pushed the sadness away, willing herself to savor this moment while it was still here. She would face the loneliness later, after he'd left. For now, all she could do was lace her arm around his chest and hug him tight.

RANULF POUNDED on the cottage door once more, but still there was no answer. Maerwynn must be up at her garden, or mayhap milking her cow. With any luck, he'd find her alone, without that bastard Scot around to interfere.

He rounded the corner of the hut, squinting up at the gardens. But he saw no sign of her. Trudging up the hillside, he scanned the sloping landscape. His gaze snagged on a flash of red off to the right, near where the freshwater stream tumbled by.

Maerwynn. That blaze of hair was unmistakable. He hurried forward, but as he crested a small rise, what he saw stopped him in his tracks.

She and the Scot were bare as the day they were born in the grass. Limbs entangled, they lay in repose, the Scot idly combing her hair with his fingers and Maerwynn tucked securely against his chest.

Ranulf stumbled back, the air rushing from his lungs. He scrambled down the slope somewhat, ducking behind a windswept shrub to avoid being seen. While he caught his breath, he groped to make sense of what he'd just seen.

Though neither had stirred, it was clear what they had just done. Their limbs were heavy with satisfaction, and they made no attempt to hide their nakedness. His stomach curdled with hatred.

The whore.

She would freely give that man, a stranger and a Scot, no less, what she so willfully denied Ranulf? Aye, she played the part of an innocent well, pushing Ranulf away and reminding him of his blasted wife Jeanet. But all the while, she was teasing him, dangling herself in front of him and then scampering into the arms of that savage, barbaric—

The hot rage boiling in his blood turned to icy comprehension. He'd been far too generous with her, thinking that she would play her part, even if it took a bit of…*coaxing* on his end. She should have been grateful to him for all he'd done for her. She should have been falling all over herself at the chance to be his mistress.

But she was an unthankful bitch, willful and reckless. She *owed* Ranulf, yet she'd rutted with some other man like the wanton whore she was.

He'd shown her too much mercy in the hopes that she would understand her debt to him and acquiesce to his wishes. And this was the thanks he got.

He should have let the loudest and most riled villagers finish both her and her grandmother off all those years ago. This was *his* domain, after all. He would not be played a fool, nor cast aside by some headstrong harlot.

The bitter thought sparked a seed of an idea. Mayhap there was still a way to be rid of her. It would take some doing on his part, but the effort would be worth it if it meant teaching her a lesson and eradicating her vile presence from his life.

Rising from behind the bush, he backed away slowly until he was sure the cottage blocked him from Maerwynn and the Scot's view. He scuttled across the beach to his waiting boat and hastily launched it into the strait. There was no time to waste in setting his plan in motion.

Chapter Twelve

※

Nay. It was too soon.
Only a day and a half had passed since Falcon had lain with Maerwynn in the most intimate encounter of his life. Yet from the plot of land above the cottage, he could clearly see Alice's small boat scrape against the island's beach.

After rising from beside the stream, they'd spent the day attending to Maerwynn's chores. Though they'd been largely silent as they'd tended the garden, hauled water, and saw to Biddy, it was as if an invisible string connected them, keeping them from ever drifting too far apart.

And last night, Maerwynn had beckoned Falcon into her loft, where he'd held her through the dark hours, breathing in the scent of her hair and memorizing the feel of her skin beneath his hands. In the wee hours of the morning, they'd made love again, slower this time. He'd wanted to savor every moment, fearful that it might be their last.

Though he'd hoped to have several more days with her before Alice returned, some deeper intuition that their time was nearly through had proven true.

And now Alice was here. Which meant it was time for Falcon to depart.

His gaze skittered to Maerwynn. She'd straightened from the patch of earth she'd been working to stare at the beach. From the grim set to her mouth, she'd seen Alice, too.

Slowly, they both made their way down from the garden and toward the beach. No words passed between them—what was there to say?

They reached the cottage at the same moment Alice did. Yet something was amiss. As usual, the girl's big blue eyes were rounded, but her gaze was fixed on Maerwynn this time instead of Falcon. Her pale skin was flushed crimson from her hasty scramble up the beach, and her lip was caught between her teeth.

"Alice, what is it?" Maerwynn asked with a frown. "What is wrong?"

"It's Beatrice," Alice panted. "She's grown much worse since yesterday."

"Come inside and explain everything."

Falcon followed the two women into the cottage. While Alice shifted from foot to foot in the center of the room, Falcon leaned against one wall, listening.

"Has her coughing increased?" Maerwynn asked. "Or is she bringing up blood?"

"Nay, it's not her cough. She's been vomiting, and she says her tongue has grown numb. Just before I left to fetch you, she said her skin was crawling, like she was covered in ants."

Falcon's gut tightened with unease. He knew little of healing, but this was clearly a serious turn, and apparently entirely unrelated to a dry, lingering cough.

Maerwynn's brows lowered and her gaze wandered in thought. "That doesn't make sense. The horehound concoction I made was pure, and none of the ingredients would cause such a severe reaction, even if she couldn't tolerate them well. When did all this begin?"

"Yesterday evening," Alice replied. "She came to see me this morning. Naught that I gave her to ease her stomach helped, and she was growing worse. I-I didn't know what to do besides fetch you."

Maerwynn's troubled gaze focused on Alice, and she gave the girl's arm a reassuring squeeze. "You did the right thing."

Alice looked unconvinced. "She…she didn't want to see you. She seems fearful of receiving your help."

"Why?" Maerwynn breathed, clearly baffled.

Even before Alice answered, Falcon had a dark suspicion what she was about to say.

The girl wrung her hands in her skirts. "The whole village knew that Beatrice had come to see you two days past, and that you'd given her a remedy. Word spread quickly that she'd taken a turn for the worse. There are…whispers. Speculation."

"What kind of speculation?" Falcon demanded, pushing off the wall. He feared he already knew the answer based on all Maerwynn had shared of her past, but he would hear it straight from Alice.

Alice ducked her head, unwilling to meet either of their gazes. Her ears blazed red and her voice came out small when she finally spoke. "The word 'witch' has been spoken."

Falcon muttered a curse. "Fools and ungrateful rubes."

For her part, Maerwynn let a long breath go. Her features were surprisingly calm, given what Alice had just said.

But it seemed there was more, for Alice continued to gnaw on her lip. "A few are even calling for action to be taken, to protect the rest of the village. Ranulf has done naught to quell them—in fact, I heard from Widow Gelda that he was encouraging such ideas."

"*Swindon?*" Falcon barked, making Alice jump. "That man cannot seem to keep his arse where it belongs—away from ye, Maerwynn."

"It doesn't matter."

Maerwynn's words, spoken flat and quiet, stunned him.

"What does that mean?"

She lifted her gaze to his. Her eyes were stormy, yet he could not miss the resignation in their depths.

"It doesn't matter what they say. Beatrice needs me. I'm going to help her."

"Alice," Falcon said, keeping his gaze locked with Maerwynn's. "Would ye mind giving us a moment alone? I need to discuss something in private with Maerwynn."

Alice was all too eager to scurry out of the cottage and close the door tight behind her.

Alone, all Falcon wanted to do was go to Maerwynn—take her in his arms and shake some sense into her. Or mayhap just hold her close and keep her safe from the outside world.

But her wellbeing wasn't his concern anymore. He couldn't stay, and she couldn't leave. All he could do was hope to talk her out of a dangerous decision.

"Ye'd be mad to go to Edelby now. Swindon and the others will whip themselves into a frenzy of fear and suspicion. The situation could get out of hand quickly."

"What would you have me do, then?" she demanded. "Stay here at my leisure while Beatrice grows worse or mayhap even dies? I have a responsibility to the people of Edelby, Falcon."

"Even if they mean to hurt ye? Ye cannot be so blind as to ignore the danger. Ye do not owe them yer life, lass."

She crossed her arms stubbornly over her chest, her jaw clamping shut. It seemed they were at an impasse.

But Falcon wasn't willing to give up on her just yet. A half-formed idea bubbled up in his mind.

"What if…" Aye, this might actually work. "What if ye came with me?"

She blinked slowly. "What?"

"Come with me." He took a hobbling step forward, the plan coalescing in his mind. "Ye could be my bride. We'd return to Arcmare together. Ye wouldn't have to deal with these small-minded fools ever again. Ye could continue on as a healer in Scotland. My father desperately needs someone with yer talent."

Maerwynn's jaw worked in disbelief for a long moment. "Is that supposed to be a proposal?"

"It would solve both our problems right now. I would have a bride, and ye could continue yer work someplace where ye'd be safe and truly valued. It is practical."

Falcon knew as the words left his mouth that he was making a mess of this. He was going about it all wrong, yet he couldn't seem to right things.

Maerwynn's face turned stony. Damn him.

Tell her ye care for her! a voice screamed in the back of his head. *Tell her ye cannot be apart from her. Aught else besides the practical, ye cowardly arse.*

Why wouldn't the words come? The thought of being vulnerable, of baring his feelings to her, made his throat close and his chest tighten. He didn't know how to lower his defenses, not after a life spent building them up. All he'd learned from the time he'd been born was how to fight, how to win, how to toughen himself alongside his brother.

Standing before Maerwynn now, he knew with keen clarity how hollow his life had been before her—and how hollow it would be after. If only she would see reason and come with him. If only she could see right into his heart and comprehend the truth there, even though he couldn't bring himself to say it.

Instead, she looked at him with eyes like a frosted-over sea. "That would be convenient for you, wouldn't it? You'd have your bride and you'd win your little competition. And after, what of me? I suppose you'd set me aside once I'd worn out my usefulness."

"Nay, it wouldn't be like—"

Liquid hurt filled her eyes. "Of course, you'd let me stay on as a servant to your father. That is quite the offer."

Aye, he could see how his cold words sounded, but the urge to defend the notion of taking her someplace where she would be treasured rather than reviled for her healing abilities swelled within him.

"Think of yer safety, Maerwynn. Think of the constant threat ye live under here. It could be different."

"And you think simply abandoning Edelby and Gull Island will solve all my problems?"

"Aye."

"I don't know why I'm surprised. You've made it clear from the moment you arrived that you always look for the shortcut, the fastest and easiest way to what you want. That was how you intended to find a bride, and how you hoped your leg would recover."

She lifted her chin, her gaze shimmering with stubborn pride. "But I am not like you. Some things are worth fighting for, struggling for. I'll not cut my losses and run from my problems. I mean to keep my promise to my grandmother, and to those in Edelby. I'm staying."

"But what about—"

Her cool exterior shattered then. She flung her arms to her sides, her whole body going taut. "Don't you see? What you offer is no better than what I have here. If I want to be useful but unwanted, and set aside so as not to be a bother to anyone, I could simply stay here on the island. I may never be lucky enough to marry, but if I do, I want it to be for love, not convenience or show. But you see me the same way they all do—a means to your own ends, naught more. You're no different than the villagers—or Ranulf."

He took a jerking step back, barely remembering to catch himself on his crutch.

It was better this way, he told himself grimly. It was easier to leave knowing that she hated him now.

"Very well," he said, his voice like gravel. "I'll leave ye be, then."

He glanced around the hut, but he had no possessions to gather, naught to take with him but bittersweet memories.

"We'd best make haste to Edelby," he offered, no longer able to look her in the eyes. "Beatrice needs ye, and I might as well use the last few hours of daylight to secure passage to Carlisle."

She swallowed hard, and he thought for a moment that she would fall apart. Instead, she gave him a curt nod and swept out the door, leaving him alone with his battered heart.

Chapter Thirteen

Silence as heavy as an anvil hung over the boat ride to Edelby. Alice had clearly intuited the mood between Maerwynn and Falcon, and wisely kept quiet.

For her part, Maerwynn cloaked herself in cool composure, but it felt as though her insides had turned to shards of glass.

How had everything gone so wrong? She'd known from the start that Falcon was going to leave. She could only blame herself for letting emotion grow for him.

Even still, his "proposal" had been like a dagger to her heart. He saw her as a solution, the perfect showwife. She was an easy path to victory for him, naught more. He didn't care for her. And despite his promises of comfort and safety in his little arrangement, he hadn't offered the one thing she longed for more than aught else—love.

She was a fool to have hoped for more. Worse, she had even considered his offer for a fleeting second. But she saw clearly now. She was fated to be alone forever.

Struggling against that fate only brought pain and despair.

When the boat bumped into the village's wooden docks, Falcon hoisted himself out with the aid of his crutch and helped Alice and Maerwynn disembark. His strong hands around her waist were warm and soothing, but they vanished as soon as her feet were planted on the dock.

"Where can I procure a horse?" he asked Alice stiffly.

Alice shot a round-eyed gaze between Maerwynn and Falcon. "Tad Williamson runs the stables at the edge of the village," she said, pointing. "Just beyond those trees."

"Thank ye." Falcon turned to Maerwynn then. "May I have a word?"

"Do not make this more difficult than it already is," she replied softly.

But even before Maerwynn could take Alice's arm and walk away, the girl darted off down the dock. "I'll be at Beatrice's," she called over her shoulder. "She is in the same cottage as before you left, beside the butcher's."

Her reinforcement fleeing, Maerwynn cast her gaze about at anything other than Falcon's large form before her.

"I only wanted to say thank ye," he murmured.

Her restraint dissolved like salt in warm water. She met his gaze. His eyes were gentle as they traced her face.

"Ye saved my life. And this last fortnight has

been…" His throat bobbed and a muscle twitched in his jaw. "I will never forget ye, lass."

"Nor I," she managed to whisper.

There was so much more to say, so much left unexplored between them. Yet her throat had constricted so tightly that even her breath came with difficulty.

His hand rose to cup her cheek, the rough pads of his fingers playing along her jawline. For a heart-stopping moment, she thought he would kiss her, but instead, he pulled his hand away and let it fall.

"Thank ye again."

She opened her mouth to say something, anything, but he was already turning away. She stared at his broad back as he crutched off in the direction Alice had pointed until he became a blurry smudge through her tears.

It felt as though her chest had been cracked open and her heart laid bare to the elements. She desperately wanted to crumple to the dock's wooden planks and weep.

But she needed to hold herself together just a little longer. She could fall apart later, when she was back in her cottage once more, alone, ensconced on her island prison. Right now, Beatrice still needed tending, and if Alice's description had been accurate, the woman was in grave danger.

Dashing the heels of her hands under her eyes and drawing a fortifying breath, Maerwynn willed her feet into motion.

It was strange to be in Edelby again after ten years away. There were more boats moored at the docks, and the huts seemed more tightly packed than before, but otherwise, little had changed. The dock spit her onto the town's main street, which was lined with shop signs she recognized, though all the windows had been shuttered now that twilight was setting in.

She wound her way along the street, turning once she'd passed the hanging sign with a flank of meat to indicate the butcher's shop. A narrow alley led her to Beatrice's cottage. Low light slipped out around the shutters—hopefully a sign that Beatrice was still alive inside.

Maerwynn knocked once but didn't wait for a response. Instead, she let herself in directly, unwilling to waste time with pleasantries when every moment might count.

Beatrice lay on a cot before the hearth, her skin slicked with sweat and her whole body trembling. Alice bent over her, mopping her brow with a damp cloth. The girl lifted her head at Maerwynn's entrance, her pale blonde eyebrows knitted together.

"She had deteriorated further," Alice murmured, stepping aside so that Maerwynn could get a closer look.

At first, Maerwynn suspected a pestilent fever like the one that had stolen her mother, given Beatrice's shivering. But when she laid a hand across the woman's forehead, her skin was not warm to the touch. Mayhap not a plague or spreading illness, then.

"Tell me what you feel, Beatrice," Maerwynn asked in her gentle but firm healer's voice.

Beatrice's clouded brown gaze focused on her for a moment, and she recoiled into the cot. "*You.*"

Maerwynn's jaw tightened. "I am here to help. Now tell me where and how you are most pained."

Beatrice continued to stare hard at Maerwynn, but her suffering must have been great enough to frighten her into speaking.

"M-my stomach. It burns."

Had she ingested something? Maerwynn would stake her life on the safety of the horehound concoction she'd made for the woman—in fact, with every remedy she produced, she ran the risk of returning accusations of witchcraft and malfeasance, so she always had to be careful that her treatments were reliable and safe.

"What have you eaten in the last day or two?" she asked. "Uncooked meat, mayhap, or did you pick something beyond the village without recognizing it?"

"N-nay."

"Did you drink water from a stagnant pool?"

"Nay." Beatrice grimaced and clutched her stomach, pain contorting her face. "I cannot feel my tongue. Please, I beg of you, remove your curse, witch."

Despite all her years of training, Maerwynn stumbled back a step at that, her mind reeling.

"I would never harm—"

It didn't matter. Beatrice had turned her attention to scratching at her arms and chest. Naught Maerwynn said now would get through to her. Besides, it wasn't her job to convince Beatrice of her innocence. She needed to find a solution to the woman's ailment, and fast.

But even as she sifted through all the possibilities, no explanation presented itself. The mysterious illness had come on not long after Beatrice's visit to the island, but

Maerwynn's horehound drops were perfectly safe. Beatrice claimed not to have eaten or drank anything tainted, and nor did she appear to have a spreading sickness.

A loud thumping on the door broke her chain of thought and made both her and Alice jump.

"Maerwynn Thorne," a male voice shouted from outside. "We know you're in there."

Maerwynn's gaze shot to Alice, whose eyes were round as the moon.

"Come out and answer for what you've done to Beatrice!"

Heaven help her. Despite Alice's warning, Maerwynn hadn't truly believed the situation had grown so perilous.

She'd made a grave misjudgment.

Chapter Fourteen

Falcon used every drop of self-control not to reach out and throttle Tad Williamson.

"I've explained it to ye twice before. This will be the last time. I am an Earl's son. I was shipwrecked. Nay, I don't have any coin to pay ye with now. But once I reach Arcmare, I will send ye double what yer best animal is worth."

The stablemaster continued to give him a wary look. "So you've claimed."

If Falcon were thinking rationally, he could admit that he was a Scottish outsider, his clothes were rather tattered, and he had naught more valuable than his wooden crutch to his name. The Englishman across from him had no cause to trust or believe him.

The problem was, he wasn't thinking rationally. He was thinking like a man mad with a broken heart. Which he was. Saying farewell to Maerwynn had been like giving up air. He needed her, damnit.

And yet here he stood, making a fool of himself in search of a horse.

Tad eyed him for another moment, then grudgingly turned to the long row of stalls behind him.

"Let me see what I can part with," he grumbled over his shoulder.

No doubt Falcon would be riding away on the oldest, most cantankerous nag in all of England.

What the hell was he doing? He tilted his head back and stared up at the rapidly darkening sky.

He'd been over this more times than he could count, and he simply couldn't find a solution. If he didn't leave with all haste, he would be forfeiting his father's lands and title to River. As it was, he might have already lost, but he still couldn't simply remain here and give up his entire life at Arcmare. Could he?

And despite his proposal, Maerwynn refused to leave this cursed place, which meant if he wanted to be with her, he'd have to stay.

You always look for the shortcut, the fastest and easiest way to what you want.

Her chastising words rang through his head. Aye, he'd proposed—a marriage of convenience. But was that even truly what he wanted? Or was it simply easier to speak of his feelings for her as if they were neat and tidy rather than messy and all-consuming?

Some things are worth fighting for, struggling for.

Falcon had never been afraid to fight, at least not physically. Then why was he running from this—from *her*—like a coward?

God almighty, he was being such a fool, fearing what

was right in front of him all along—real love. It wasn't clean. It wasn't easy. And it certainly wasn't what he'd set out to find. But he couldn't deny it any longer. He'd fallen in love with Maerwynn. With her beauty and strength, her iron will and her fragile heart.

She was right, blast it all. There were no shortcuts or quick solutions when it came to their dilemma. But how could he dream of letting her go? This wasn't some game or competition to be won. This was his life. And he couldn't live it without her.

It was past time he give up his pride and his stubborn insistence on beating his brother. If it meant living on Gull Island to be with Maerwynn, then so be it.

If she'd have him. God, he'd made a mess of things with her. But mayhap if he told her the truth, confessed the surprising love that had grown in his heart, he could win back her trust. And mayhap, if he was the luckiest bastard in the world, she could love him, too.

Tad re-emerged from the stables then, dragging an ancient, sway-backed speckled mare behind him.

"Forget the horse," Falcon said. "Apologies for yer trouble, but I am not leaving this night."

The stablemaster leveled him with a withering glare, muttering about no-good, bothersome Scots.

Just as Tad turned to haul the poor old beast back to her stall, a man carrying a torch came running from the direction of the village.

"Tad! You won't want to miss this." The man skidded to a halt, panting. He cast Falcon a curious glance, but then returned his attention to the stablemaster. "The witch is *here*. Constable Swindon has gathered some men and we intend to run her off—or be rid of her by other means if she will not go quietly."

Cold fear stabbed through Falcon's chest like a blade. *Maerwynn*. She was in danger, and at the hands of that bastard Swindon again.

Without thinking, he snatched the torch from the villager's hand.

"Oi!" The man made to grab it back, but Falcon drew back his fist and leveled him with a single blow to the stomach. The man crumpled to the ground with a wheeze and a grunt.

"Go home," Falcon ordered. "Ye will only regret any trouble ye cause this night. Understand?" The villager on the ground gave a weak nod. Falcon swung the torch toward Tad, who also bobbed his head before retreating back into the stables.

Sparing them not another thought, Falcon barreled off toward the village as fast as his crutch would allow. Dull pain in his leg be damned. He needed to get to Maerwynn. *Now*.

Chapter Fifteen

"Come out or we'll break down the door!"

Maerwynn had tried to stall the gathering mob outside. Then she'd attempted to reason with them through the door. The fact was, Beatrice was deteriorating rapidly, and she and Alice had naught but water and rags to treat her. If they were going to reach Alice's supplies on the other side of the village, there was only one option left.

She had to face them.

Maerwynn turned to Alice. "Remember, they want me, not you. If things take a turn…" She swallowed hard. "Try to stay out of the way, and get to your hut. Mayhap fetch some marjoram for Beatrice's stomach, and cloves to ease her pain."

She shook her head in frustration. They needed to get to the bottom of Beatrice's ailment, but she couldn't think with the villagers hollering and banging outside.

Alice gave her a frightened nod. Straightening her spine, Maerwynn moved to the door and lifted the bar she'd fitted over it when the mob had first started pounding. When she drew the door open, she had to will herself not to take a step back.

At least twenty men had gathered outside. Several held torches to illuminate the night. Their features were twisted with suspicion and displeasure in the flickering light.

And at their front was Ranulf.

A surprised hush fell over the crowd at her sudden appearance, but then someone in the back shouted, "Devil's handmaid!" and a ripple of mutters rose up.

Ranulf lifted his hand for order. "Let us deal with this disturbance of the peace calmly, men."

"Disturbance of the peace?" Maerwynn replied. "I have done naught except attempt to treat a sick woman."

"You broke the accord you agreed to ten years past by setting foot on mainland soil," Ranulf said, his voice flat yet his blue eyes piercing as they fixed on her.

Another man—Hamond Gilroy, a fisher, if Maerwynn remembered correctly—pushed his way up beside Ranulf. "That is only a sliver of the matter at hand, Constable. How did Beatrice fall ill in the first place? This…*woman* had something to do with it."

Several "ayes" echoed through the crowd.

"Indeed, Hamond, that is what we must determine," Ranulf replied.

Oh, God. Before she'd even realized what was happening, Maerwynn found herself in the midst of a trial—with her at the center.

"The facts are these," Ranulf continued, taking on

an air of impartial authority. "Beatrice went to Gull Island two days past for a cough remedy. The next day, she fell gravely ill, not with a cough, but with a foul stomach and trembling limbs."

"I gave her a mixture of honey, lemon balm, and horehound for her throat," Maerwynn said, raising her voice to be heard over the crowd. "All are innocuous."

"Ah, but this doesn't just concern your present actions, does it?" Ranulf frowned as if his next words saddened him to speak. "This is also about the past, and the rumors that seem to keep cropping up."

Rumors that Ranulf himself had stoked, according to Alice. Maerwynn seethed inside. Intuition told her that Ranulf was manipulating the situation in some way. Mayhap he sought to back her into a corner and force her to agree to be his mistress.

Who knew, but she couldn't just accuse the Constable of some vendetta against her before half the village. They would likely think she was just deflecting, attempting to smear Ranulf's name to divert attention from herself.

The mob, riled by Ranulf's words, began rumbling again. "Witch!" someone hissed. "She brings evil with her, I swear!" another muttered.

"I am a healer," Maerwynn yelled over the rising din. "I have devoted my life to saving lives and helping—"

They weren't listening to her anymore. The shouted accusations were growing louder. When she turned to Ranulf, she caught a little smile on his lips before he schooled his features into sober concern once more. He held up his hand again, and the crowd grudgingly quieted somewhat.

"Mayhap it would be best if you...removed yourself, Maerwynn. And not just to Gull Island this time. You are clearly no longer welcome here."

Sudden tears burned behind her eyes. This was her home. Where else was she supposed to go? Alone and with naught but a few dried herbs and an old milk cow to her name, how was she supposed to start over in a new town?

"Nay," she choked out. "I will not be driven away from my home. I made a promise to stay and look after you all, even if you hate me."

Hamond snatched a torch from a man standing next to him. He leaned over Maerwynn, the firelight catching his dark eyes. "If you will not go peacefully, mayhap we ought to be rid of you some other way."

Maerwynn backed up until she bumped into Beatrice's wooden door. She'd thought there was still a chance to reason with the villagers, but as they cheered at Hamond's dark threat, she realized just how wrong she'd been.

Heart hammering in her ears, she turned a desperate gaze on Ranulf. Though he might enjoy seeing her suffer a bit if it meant she'd be left no choice but to seek his protection—and his bed—he was still the Constable. He had to keep order. Why wasn't he stopping the calls to string her up or toss her onto a bonfire?

When his gaze met hers, the cold malice shining in his eyes sent a chill into her bones. Could he actually *want* to see her hurt or even killed? She knew he was a power-hungry man, but there was clearly more to it than that now.

In the corner of her eye, she caught a flash of white-blonde hair as Alice darted off through the crowd. Good. At least she would be safe from the mob that so obviously wanted blood.

"Ranulf, please!" Maerwynn shouted, hoping against hope to put a stop to the villagers' rising fervor.

His only reply was to lift one shoulder at her, a smug, hateful look settling over his face.

"We are all in danger if she remains!" someone cried. "Let us be rid of the witch!" The shouts grew louder and the crowd began to shift closer.

"Halt!" The single voice cut through the others like a clap of thunder.

Falcon!

Several heads whipped around to seek the source of the booming order.

Falcon stood at the back of the crowd, a torch held high in one hand. Though he leaned on his crutch, he cut a powerful figure through the night.

"If any one of ye men attempts to harm her, ye'll have to go through me."

He moved toward her and positioned himself between her and the mob.

"This doesn't concern you, stranger," Hamond said, glaring at Falcon.

Falcon shoved his torch at one of the men standing nearby so that he could cross his arms over his chest. "Och, aye, it does if it involves Maerwynn."

Ranulf took a step forward, blue fire in his eyes as he

stared Falcon down. "She is a danger to this village. She was given the opportunity to leave but refused. You have no authority here, Scot. Move, or you will be moved."

"Try it."

Ranulf rolled his eyes and made to turn away, but then suddenly he darted forward, snaking an arm out to grab Maerwynn.

Like lightning, Falcon spun his crutch in his hand and rapped Ranulf across the knuckles with it as if it were a staff. Ranulf yelped in pain and yanked his hand back, clutching it to his chest. A murmur of shock went through those gathered.

"I am the Constable of this village!" Ranulf screamed. "You will obey me, or…" His good hand shifted to his waist, where his sword hung.

Please, nay. Besides his crutch, Falcon had no weapon. Even if it were a fair fight otherwise, the odds would be against Falcon given his still-healing leg. And there were twenty other enraged men behind Ranulf, eager for their turn against the outsider.

Just then, Alice came skidding back into the circle of light cast by the torches.

"Alice, don't—"

But the girl didn't heed Maerwynn's desperate warning to stay away. Instead, she plowed into the crowd, pushing her way to the front. When she reached Maerwynn and Falcon, she turned to those gathered.

Her hand shot into the air. It looked as though she clenched some crumpled plant matter wrapped in a rag.

"Monkshood!"

Everyone was so caught off guard by the strange

sequence of events that the crowd fell silent, staring dumbfounded at Alice.

"Is…is that a hex or curse?" someone whispered uncertainly.

Realization crashed through Maerwynn's mind.

"Nay," she said, her voice rising. "It's another name for wolfsbane—*poison*."

Chapter Sixteen

Pandemonium broke out at Maerwynn's words. Several men recoiled from both her and Alice, who still held the plant matter aloft. Others shouted in confusion or disbelief. Some even hissed that it was more evil-doing by the witch.

But Falcon knew the truth. Comprehension forked through him like a bolt of lightning on the heels of the revelation about the wolfsbane.

His gaze shot to Ranulf Swindon. The man's cold blue eyes had gone wide and his nostrils flared, but then he hastily attempted to school his features. His motivations for fanning the flames of hysteria against Maerwynn were beyond Falcon, but Swindon had clearly sought to frame her with the poison.

"Beatrice's abrupt turn for the worse," Maerwynn murmured, still assembling the pieces. "Her symptoms—numb tongue, crawling skin, sweating, and a racing pulse. Of course. Wolfsbane explains them all."

Her gaze shot to Alice. "Where did you find that?"

Alice gingerly lowered the crumpled plants, careful to keep them wrapped in the rag. "On the rubbish heap right behind Constable Swindon's cottage."

Another wave of confusion passed through the crowd. Several sets of eyes turned to Swindon.

Before the others could voice their questions, Ranulf jumped in.

"The girl likely put them there at Maerwynn's behest. She's lying!"

"Nay, I'm not," Alice shot back. "While all of you were busy attacking Maerwynn for trying to help, Beatrice has been lying inside, growing worse by the moment. I ran to my hut in hopes of finding something to treat her. When I took the shortcut through the alleyway behind the cobbler's shop, I passed by the rear of the Constable's home. These plants are unmistakable if you know what they are."

Ranulf took a step toward Alice, but Falcon moved faster, angling so that he blocked both Maerwynn and the girl. Swindon was forced to draw back, but he pointed an accusatory finger at Alice.

"She apprentices for Maerwynn. Mayhap they are both responsible for the wickedness in this village."

A large, dark-haired villager shifted forward, a frown on his coarse features. From the size of the arms crossed over his chest, he was likely the village blacksmith.

"Alice is a good girl," he said, to murmurs of agreement from several others. "Aye, she has learned about healing from Maerwynn, but she has used that knowledge to help many of us with minor ailments in the last few years. Not one of us can say any ill has come from her remedies."

More nods followed the man's words. Maerwynn's gaze shifted to Alice, emotion filling her eyes.

"What I want to know," someone else said from deeper in the crowd, "is why poison—wolfsbane or monkshood or whatever the hell it's called—was used on Beatrice."

"And why those leaves and such were on the Constable's rubbish heap," another man added.

Several "ayes" rumbled through those gathered.

"Mayhap," Falcon ventured, meeting the men's confused gazes, "yer Constable wanted to turn ye against Maerwynn—whip ye into a frenzy to drive her out, or worse."

He was met with surprise but not outright hostility.

"Why would he do that?" someone called.

"Aye, that would be barbaric."

"Not like a keeper of the peace."

"I do not know why," Falcon responded. "But I witnessed Swindon trying to kiss Maerwynn. She rejected him, even when he grew rough with her."

Shock rippled through those gathered, and more eyes turned to Swindon.

Swindon must have sensed that he was losing control of the situation. His gaze darted over the men before him. "This man is an outsider—a Scot. Naught he says can be believed. He is trying to smear my good name because he has lain with that whore!" He jabbed a finger toward Maerwynn.

White-hot rage flashed through Falcon's veins.

Ranulf must have seen Falcon and Maerwynn together. That had to be the root behind Ranulf's attack on Maerwynn now. He wanted her for himself, and when he finally saw that he couldn't have her, he'd sought to destroy her completely.

Falcon ached to drive his fist into Swindon's foul mouth for besmirching Maerwynn before the village, but instead he clenched his hands at his sides. The last thing he needed was to dissolve into a rage, casting the whole situation into chaos. Nay, he needed to remain cool-headed. Maerwynn's very life depended upon it.

Confusion broke out at Swindon's accusation, but Falcon lifted a calm voice over the noise.

"Aye, I am an outsider—which means I can see the situation clearer. I did not know Maerwynn—or Alice, or Swindon—until recently. I watched her treat Beatrice with care and attention. I saw Swindon's anger and embarrassment when she rejected him. And now I've seen and heard what Alice has discovered."

Falcon paused, glancing about those gathered. Though many wore frowns, he had their attention.

"It is not my place to tell ye all what to do in yer own village," he continued evenly. "But I can tell ye this much. Swindon wants to make ye his puppets, pull yer strings and have ye do his bidding. He wants ye to carry out his ill will against an innocent woman. If I were ye, I wouldn't like being played the fool in such a manner."

That stunned the villagers into silence for a long moment. Then several began to nod slowly.

The big man who'd spoken earlier cleared his throat. "This matter clearly isn't as simple as we all thought.

Mayhap we'd all best return home and let things be for the night. Tomorrow morn, cooler heads will prevail. Besides, Beatrice still needs help, and none of us ought to stand in Maerwynn and Alice's way."

He turned stiffly to Swindon. "And Constable, mayhap it would be best if you stayed the night at my forge."

Swindon worked his jaw in disbelief. "Why?" he demanded. "I have done naught wrong. And you are not the keeper of the peace here, Arnold. I am."

"I only wish to keep an eye on you for the night," the man, Arnold, replied quietly. "Besides, I think we'll all have some questions for you come first light."

Ranulf slunk back from the crowd, his eyes shooting about for an ally. But the flat, hard stares of the villagers were all that met him.

"If it was wolfsbane that made Beatrice ill, what can you do for her, Mistress?" Arnold asked, shifting his attention to Maerwynn.

She seemed stunned by the earnest question for a moment, but then her features pinched in thought. She opened her mouth to respond, yet it was Swindon's low voice that cut through the silence.

"Nay," he hissed. "You will not win. This is *my* village, whore, not yours."

He had backed away from the crowd and into the shadows, his hunched form murky. But the whisper of his blade as it came free from its scabbard was unmistakable.

Like a shot arrow, Ranulf lunged forward. His sword

flashed in the torchlight as it plunged through the air—straight for Maerwynn.

"Nay!"

On instinct, Falcon dove between Ranulf's sword and Maerwynn. Time seemed to slow as the distance between the blade's savage point and his chest halved, then halved again. His mind went quiet, stripped of its ability to keep pace. In that instant, his wits ceded control to his body.

He moved as if he'd faced this exact situation a thousand times. He *had* faced something similar at least once, when he'd been sparring with River. Unlike then, he didn't have a wooden practice sword to deflect the incoming blow, but he did have his crutch.

Just as he had that day a few years ago on the training lists with River, Falcon caught Ranulf's sword with his crutch, then swept a large circle with his wrist to take control of the blade's trajectory.

Ranulf's momentum carried him forward even as the blade's hilt was pried from his hand. Falcon saw his window of opportunity. He torqued the sword free and into his own free hand, then spun the blade to bring its tip around to face Ranulf.

Swindon did not draw up, though. His rage-filled gaze remained locked on Maerwynn as he plunged forward with a savage bellow. His roar was cut short as he impaled himself on the end of his own sword, now held in Falcon's hand.

Sagging to the ground, Ranulf stared down in confusion at the blade in his belly. Falcon withdrew the sword and tossed it aside with an oath. Maerwynn rushed forward, but even before she reached the ground, Swindon had already slumped to one side, his eyes growing glassy as his life's blood left him.

Falcon caught her before she crumpled to her knees in shock. She shook in his grasp like a leaf in high wind.

"He was…he meant to…if you hadn't stopped him…"

"Hush, lass."

A stunned silence had fallen over the crowd of villagers. Still holding Maerwynn in his arms, he turned to them.

"I didn't intend to kill the man," he said quietly. "But I couldn't let him hurt Maerwynn."

Arnold swiped a shaky hand over his face. "We all saw what happened. You acted in defense of Maerwynn's life. Still, I'd best get word to the Sheriff. Mayhap you ought to stay in Edelby for a few days, just until he can speak with you."

"Aye, I'll stay, but on Gull Island, not in the village."

Arnold nodded thoughtfully, his gaze absorbing the sight of Maerwynn in Falcon's arms before he turned to a few of the other villagers. "Help me get Swindon's body out of the street."

Falcon rotated so that Maerwynn wouldn't have to see Ranulf anymore. Yet she pulled back in his hold slightly, looking up at him with distraught eyes.

"You are going back to the island?"

"Aye, I'll take ye home."

"But Beatrice—"

"I know what to do," Alice said, stepping forward.

Maerwynn blinked. "You do?"

"Aye. She needs a dose of foxglove."

Despite his complete trust in Maerwynn, and by association her apprentice, Falcon stiffened. "Isn't that poisonous also?"

Alice turned her owlish eyes on him. "Indeed, but in the right dose, it can counteract the wolfsbane. Foxglove slows the heart—or stops it altogether if too much is given. But against wolfsbane, which speeds the heart and makes its beat erratic, foxglove can stabilize the pulse while the wolfsbane is purged."

Maerwynn made a little noise of surprise. "That's exactly right."

Alice's wiry frame seemed to puff up. "I learned that from you."

Blinking against a sheen of tears, Maerwynn took on the healer's tone Falcon was now familiar with. "Once you give the dose of foxglove, make sure she takes plenty of water and a charcoal mixture to purge the wolfsbane."

"Of course. And I'll send someone to the island if she worsens. If no one comes, trust that she made it through the night."

Maerwynn squeezed Alice's arm. "I'm so proud of you."

Again Alice swelled, her teeth sinking into her lip with modest pleasure at the praise. Mirroring the air of a healer, the girl sobered and gave Maerwynn a serious nod before hurrying off to her tasks.

Spent, Maerwynn sagged into Falcon's chest.

"Come along, lass," he said. "I'm taking ye home."

Chapter Seventeen

※

Maerwynn stirred a long time later. Warm arms held her, and soft breath rustled her hair. She lay in Falcon's arms on the mattress on her cottage's floor. Was this a dream? It felt too perfect to be real.

But somehow it was. The events of the night before came swirling back. Beatrice's frightening illness. The mob of villagers. And Ranulf's accusations.

Heaven help her, if Falcon hadn't been there…but he had been. He'd come back to her, saved her life. And then he'd sailed her back to the safety of her cottage. When she'd been too exhausted to cross the rocky beach, he'd carried her to bed.

And he'd held her all night and into the morning. Judging from the light streaming in around the shutters, it was approaching midday. Tucked in Falcon's arms, she'd slept like the dead.

"Morning." His low, groggy voice rumbled through his chest where her head rested.

She was reluctant to lose the contact, but she wanted

to look into his eyes when she said her next words. She pushed up to one elbow and caught his sleepy, dark gaze.

"Thank you, Falcon. For standing up to the villagers and facing Ranulf and…" She swallowed hard against the swell of raw emotion. "And for staying with me so that I would not have to be alone last night."

He traced her features with his eyes. "If ye'll have me, I would stay longer."

For one soaring heartbeat, she thought he meant… but nay, he'd made his priorities clear. He still had his father's lands and title to win, and a family to return to in Scotland. But he'd agreed to stay in the area until the Sheriff was summoned.

"Of course," she replied, her throat tight. "I know you will not relish the delay, but it will only be a day or two until the Sheriff arrives. And I cannot image there will be any trouble after that. The Sheriff won't be pleased one of his Constables is dead, but there were too many witnesses to Ranulf's attack to call it aught other than defense. And then…" She fought against her rapidly closing throat. "And then you can be on your way once more."

Falcon's dark brows drew together. "Nay, lass, ye misunderstand. I meant…" Now it was his turn to swallow, a muscle jumping in his jaw. "I meant I hoped to stay with ye forever."

Maerwynn pushed herself all the way to sitting. Now she must be dreaming—or hallucinating from the strain of last night. "What?"

He took her hand in his, his thumb making little

swirls over her skin. "I want to marry ye, Maerwynn. And not for show or convenience or to win some competition. I want to marry ye because I love ye with all my heart and cannot imagine another day—another moment—without ye."

"You…" Maerwynn's head spun wildly. "You cannot mean that."

"I do." A soft smile played around his lips. "I was an arse and a coward before. I wanted to marry ye just as badly as I do now, but I was afraid to admit it—afraid of the strength of the love I feel for ye. But I want ye more than aught else—more than air or water or sunshine. And I meant what I said. This isn't about my father's challenge to River and me. The Earldom be damned—it means naught, whereas ye mean everything. I would rather stay here with ye on this island for the rest of my days than live without ye as King of all Scotland."

Maerwynn's heart swelled until it felt as though her ribs could no longer contain it. She drew in a shaky breath. "I…I do not want that."

Falcon froze, his thumb and even his breath stilling. "Ye don't?"

Belatedly, she realized what he must have thought—that she was rejecting his proposal and his hope for a life with her yet again.

"I do not wish to stay on the island," she added hurriedly.

He released a wheezing breath. "Oh." Then the implication of her words hit him. "Oh?"

"I have realized something," she began, her voice

wobbling. "I was afraid, too. Afraid to let myself love you, because everyone I've ever loved has died. Afraid to let the past go, even though it felt like an anvil chained to my ankle. Afraid to leave, for fear of losing my last connection to my family. But I don't want to live in fear anymore."

She blinked against the tears that stung her eyes, determined to hold Falcon's gaze.

"I also realized last night that no matter what I do, the villagers will probably never fully trust me. Nor I them, if I'm honest. They sent me away when I was but a scared girl, with only my grandmother to stand with me. That past is like a bone that was never properly set—it has healed over somewhat, but it will never be made all the way right, nor can it truly be forgotten. I can't ever be happy here with such a past hanging over us all."

"But yer promise to yer grandmother," Falcon murmured, his brows drawn together.

"I've had time to consider that as well," Maerwynn said, a rueful smile tugging one side of her mouth. "I think I can keep my pledge to look after the villagers without needing to stay."

"Oh? How?"

"Alice." At his puzzled look, she continued. "When I took her on as an apprentice, I hadn't considered that she could fully replace me someday. It was more that several villagers wouldn't accept my help, nor would they come to the island. She was meant to treat those who remained fearful or resistant toward me. But last night proved that she could be so much more—that she already is. She is capable and knowledgeable, and most importantly, the villagers trust her."

"Aye," he said. "I saw that, too."

"If she agrees to it, she could take over all the duties as village healer. Who knows, she might even wish to live on Gull Island. I think she is ready to be out of her parents' home and on her own. She could look after Biddy and the gardens. And my promise to my grandmother would be fulfilled—I wouldn't be abandoning the villagers, I'd be leaving them in Alice's skilled hands."

Falcon tenderly tucked a lock of hair behind her ear. "And…and ye wouldn't miss this place? I know life hasn't been easy for ye here, but for better or worse, it is the only home ye've ever known."

Maerwynn searched each corner of her heart, but she knew she could answer without hesitation. "This place holds a great deal of memories, some good, some painful. Aye, it is the only home I've known so far, but that does not mean it is the only home I can ever know. And what I want more than aught else is a home with *you*. A new future, a new life with you. I love you, Falcon."

He shook his head in wonderment. "Ye'll marry me then?"

"Aye." Tears spilled down her cheeks, but she paid them no mind. "A hundred times aye."

"And you would go to Arcmare with me?"

She laughed and nodded. "Aye. It would be an honor to meet your family. But in truth, I don't care where I am, as long as you're there."

Abruptly, she found herself yanked into his lap, his mouth claiming hers in a searing kiss.

"I love ye, my wee siren," he whispered when he broke their kiss to let them both catch their breaths. "Now and forever."

Epilogue

❦

"What kept you from our bed into the wee hours of the morning, Husband?"

Falcon couldn't help but grin at the way Maerwynn had already begun picking up small Scottish ways of speaking, including the addition of "wee" to her vocabulary.

He lazily coiled a strand of flame-red hair around his finger, then used the fanned tip of it to caress her bare shoulder. Despite his teasing, she nuzzled closer under the bedcoverings.

"Did ye miss me?"

He could hear her smile. "I have grown quite accustomed to your attentions each night."

God above, he was a lucky bastard. It had only been a few weeks since they'd returned to Arcmare, yet he'd already experienced more happiness than his heart knew what to do with.

Maerwynn had taken to life at the castle like a bird

to the sky. His father had instantly taken a liking to her, along with the rest of the castle's staff.

What was more, Maerwynn and Roget had been working together to develop a treatment for his ailing lungs. She'd made a new tincture, poultice, or salve every day, tinkering with the ingredients and giving them to Roget to see what alleviated his discomfort the best. Once they'd settled on a strong-smelling balm that Roget rubbed on his chest every morning and night, he'd regained some energy and could breathe a little easier.

And somehow Falcon found himself more in love with Maerwynn with each passing day, more in awe of her abilities, her strength, and the warmth of her heart. But it wasn't until last night, when he'd spoken with River, that his happiness had been made complete.

"Apologies for leaving ye wanting, lass, but River and I had a few things to discuss," he said, still toying with her hair.

"Oh?"

"About the Earldom."

Despite all his delays, it had turned out that Falcon had completed their father's challenge first, and was therefore named the inheritor of Drumburgh's title and lands.

Just a short time ago, Falcon would have reveled in the victory, if only to have bested his brother in their greatest competition yet. But now he saw things differently, thanks to Maerwynn. The triumph seemed hollow compared to what mattered to him now—family, home, and love.

"He and I were both trained in the running of the estate, given the confusion about which of us would inherit. And we've both helped manage things as our father's health weakened. It seemed odd that only one of us would gain all, while the other got naught—neither responsibility nor reward."

"That does seem odd," she agreed. "But I thought that was the way of things in both England and Scotland—only the eldest born can inherit."

"Aye, well, for appearance's sake, mayhap," he said with a grin. "But my brother and I have never liked being told what to do. I think we've devised a solution."

Maerwynn sat up, one intrigued auburn eyebrow lifted.

"I will remain the official keeper of the title," Falcon said. "But we've agreed to split all the lands and share the decisions about the estate. For all intents and purposes, we'll manage the Earldom together."

Maerwynn beamed down at him. "A clever arrangement. You've satisfied your duty to the estate while still finding a way to preserve your relationship with your brother."

"Exactly."

Her bonny lips curled in a teasing grin then. "Are you still glad you went to all that effort to win your wee wager, then?"

Falcon snatched her around the waist and hauled her back down beside him in their bed. "Aye, my saucy wife," he growled. "For what I ended up winning was yer heart. And that is the greatest prize of all."

The End

Make sure to sign up for my newsletter to hear about all my sales, giveaways, and new releases. Plus, get exclusive content like stories, excerpts, cover reveals, and more. Sign up at www.EmmaPrinceBooks.com

Author's Note

It is one of my great joys in writing historical romance to combine a fictional romantic storyline with real historical details. Plus, it's such a treat to share not only a thrilling, passionate, and emotional love story with you, lovely readers, but to give you a glimpse at my research for this book as well.

Drumburgh, Arcmare, Edelby, and Gull Island are all fictitious places, but they were meant to be surrounded by real locations—Drumburgh lands and Arcmare Castle just on the Scottish side of the Solway Firth, and Edelby and Gull Island on the northwestern coast of England along the Irish Sea.

It is always particularly fun to write about healers, because it means dipping into the research surrounding medicinal herbs and their medieval uses. Chamomile, St. John's wort, and cloves were all used to treat pain and inflammation, marjoram to ease stomach discomfort, and mugwort for foot pain as well as women's

AUTHOR'S NOTE

ailments. Horehound was brewed into cough syrups and teas to alleviate coughs and head colds.

Though I don't have any evidence that medieval healers made cough drops, modern recipes for homemade cough drops could have easily been performed in the Middle Ages. The basic idea is to combine water, honey, sugar, and some sort of herbal flavoring (ginger or lemon balm would be tasty), bring it to a boil, stirring frequently, then when it reaches the right temperature for the right amount of time, pour the mixture into candy molds (or just a pan to be broken up later) and let it cool. Easy enough for a skilled medieval healer!

As for wolfsbane, healers would know to stay well away, as it was known as a highly dangerous poison. Also called monkshood in medieval England after the hooded shape of its flowers, just a small amount could kill an adult rapidly. Even a non-deadly dose can cause nausea and vomiting, racing pulse, numbed tongue, sweating, and a feeling of crawling skin.

Foxglove, though an equally dangerous poison, was sometimes used as an antidote to wolfsbane, as it counteracted wolfsbane's effects on the heart. But of course like many medicines, it's all in the dose.

Thank you for journeying back to the medieval era with me!

The Siren's Kiss was originally published in How to Wed a Wild Lass (A Medieval Scottish Duet). To read River's story by Kathryn Le Veque, look for The Jewel's Embrace on Amazon.

Thank You!

Thank you for taking the time to read *The Siren's Kiss* (A Medieval Scottish Romance)!

And thank you in advance for sharing your enjoyment of this book (or my other books) with fellow readers by leaving a review on Amazon. Long or short, detailed or to the point, I read all reviews and greatly appreciate you for writing one!

TEASERS FOR EMMA PRINCE'S BOOKS

Highland Bodyguards Series:

The Lady's Protector, the thrilling start to the Highland Bodyguards series, is available now on Amazon!

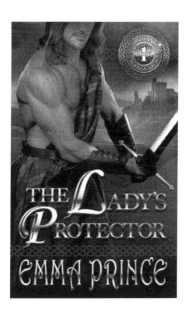

The Battle of Bannockburn may be over, but the war is far from won.

Her Protector…

Ansel Sutherland is charged with a mission from King Robert the Bruce to protect the illegitimate son of a powerful English Earl. Though Ansel bristles at aiding an Englishman, the nature of the war for Scottish independence is changing, and he is honor-bound to serve as a bodyguard. He arrives in England to fulfill his assignment, only to meet the beautiful but secretive Lady Isolda, who refuses to tell him where his ward is. When a mysterious attacker threatens Isolda's life, Ansel realizes he is the only thing standing between her and deadly peril.

His Lady...

Lady Isolda harbors dark secrets—secrets she refuses to reveal to the rugged Highland rogue who arrives at her castle demanding answers. But Ansel's dark eyes cut through all her defenses, threatening to undo her resolve. To protect her past, she cannot submit to the white-hot desire that burns between them. As the threat to her life spirals out of control, she has no choice but to trust Ansel to whisk her to safety deep in the heart of the Highlands...

The Sinclair Brothers Trilogy:

Go back to where it all began—with Robert and Alwin's story in ***Highlander's Ransom***, Book One of the Sinclair Brothers Trilogy. Available now on Amazon!

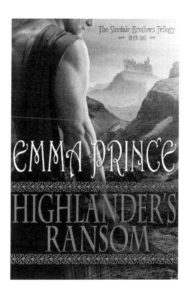

He was out for revenge…

Laird Robert Sinclair will stop at nothing to exact revenge on Lord Raef Warren, the English scoundrel who brought war to his doorstep and razed his lands and people. Leaving his clan in the Highlands to conduct covert attacks in the Borderlands, Robert lives to be a thorn in Warren's side. So when he finds a beautiful English lass on her way to marry Warren, he whisks her away to the Highlands with a plan to ransom her back to her dastardly fiancé.

She would not be controlled…

Lady Alwin Hewett had no idea when she left her father's manor to marry a man she'd never met that she would instead be kidnapped by a Highland rogue out for vengeance. But she refuses to be a pawn in any man's game. So when she learns that Robert has had them secretly wed, she will stop at nothing to regain her freedom. But her heart may have other plans…

Viking Lore Series:

Step into the lush, daring world of the Vikings with *Enthralled* (**Viking Lore, Book 1**)!

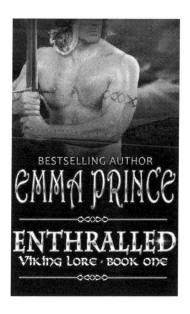

He is bound by honor…

Eirik is eager to plunder the treasures of the fabled lands to the west in order to secure the future of his village. The one thing he swears never to do is claim possession over another human being. But when he journeys across the North Sea to raid the holy houses of Northumbria, he encounters a dark-haired beauty, Laurel, who stirs him like no other. When his cruel cousin tries to take Laurel for himself, Eirik breaks his oath in an attempt to protect her. He claims her as his thrall. But can he claim her heart, or will Laurel fall prey to the devious schemes of his enemies?

She has the heart of a warrior…

Life as an orphan at Whitby Abbey hasn't been easy, but Laurel refuses to be bested by the backbreaking work and lecherous advances she must endure. When Viking raiders storm the abbey and take her captive, her strength may finally fail her—especially when she must face her fear of water at every turn. But under Eirik's gentle protection, she discovers a deeper bravery within herself—and a yearning for her golden-haired captor that she shouldn't harbor. Torn between securing her freedom or giving herself to her Viking master, will fate decide for her—and rip them apart forever?

About the Author

Emma Prince is the USA Today bestselling author of steamy historical romances jam-packed with adventure, conflict, and of course love!

Emma grew up in drizzly Seattle, but traded her rain boots for sunglasses when she and her husband moved to the eastern slopes of the Sierra Nevada. Emma spent several years in academia, both as a graduate student and an instructor of college-level English and Humanities courses. She always savored her "fun books"—normally historical romances—on breaks or vacations. But as she began looking for the next chapter in her life, she wondered if perhaps her passion could turn into a career. Ever since then, she's been reading and writing books that celebrate happily ever afters!

Emma loves connecting with readers! Sign up for her newsletter and be the first to hear about the latest book news, flash sales, giveaways, and more—signing up is free and easy at www.EmmaPrinceBooks.com.

You can follow Emma on Twitter at:
@EmmaPrinceBooks
Or join her on Facebook at:
www.facebook.com/EmmaPrinceBooks